# WRITTEN IN THE STARS

# WRITTEN IN THE STARS

A Love story Beyond destiny

ANJU DAHIYA

Srishti
Publishers & Distributors

**Srishti Publishers & Distributors**

A unit of AJR Publishing LLP

212A, Peacock Lane

Shahpur Jat, New Delhi – 110 049

editorial@srishtipublishers.com

First Published by Srishti Publishers & Distributors in 2026



10 9 8 7 6 5 4 3 2 1



Printed and bound in India.

*For my mother—*
*Who never wrote her own story,*
*but gave me the freedom to write mine.*
*Who taught me that strength lies in silence,*
*in holding a hand,*
*in simply being there.*
*And in her eyes,*
*I found all the approval I ever needed.*

## Acknowledgements

This book wouldn't have come to life without the quiet strength and constant support of my family. I want to thank my husband, Vijay, and my wonderful sons, Shivam and Adityaveer, for being my anchors, my cheerleaders, and my safe place. Your love gave me the courage to keep writing, even during the hardest days.

My gratitude to every voice, every silence, and every untold story of the people from my youth—the women who taught me strength without ever naming it; the men who stood beside or silently observed; and the moments that shaped me. You live in these pages.

Heartfelt gratitude to the team at Srishti Publishers for believing in this story and walking with me through every step of the journey. Your faith gave this book its wings.

And finally, to every reader holding this book right now—thank you for stepping into this world with me.

Yours in story and spirit,
Anju Dahiya

## Whispers Before the Story

*Some stories stay with us—*
*not because they were ours to tell,*
*but because they changed us*
*before we ever found the words.*

# Prologue

Meera tore open the envelope, expecting just another assignment. Her eyes skimmed the lines out of habit until something stopped her cold.

A name.

Familiar. Sharp. Unmistakable.

Her breath caught.

Aman Verma, IAS.

The paper crinkled slightly as her grip tightened. Could it be… him?

She read the name again. Aman Verma, IAS. Of course. How many Aman Vermas could have cleared the civil services? She told herself it could be someone else—Aman was a common name.

But logic rarely holds up against memory.

How many Aman Vermas had that kind of fire, that kind of dream?

Not many.

Her mind searched for a reason.

But memory answered first.

And memory—it never arrives like a file. It breaks in, like monsoon rain—uninvited and sudden.

It came crashing through the silence.

The smell of wet earth clinging to his shirt.

The way he used to say her name, like it was his only truth.

And then, the last time she saw him.

That look, a mix of hurt and hatred.

The kind of pain that doesn't fade.

Not with time. Not with distance.

Not even with survival.

And worst of all, the silence.

The truth she never told him.

Her hands trembled as she straightened the letter.

She had an interview to conduct.

And a past she hadn't packed away completely.

She exhaled, slowly and steadily.

Meera had always believed in meeting people in their homes—where they truly lived.

To her, interviews weren't about questions and answers.

They were about slippers left at the door.

A photo frame slightly askew on a table.

A cup of tea going cold mid-thought.

These details whispered more than any words could.

Offices were too polished, too prepared.

But homes?

Homes had truth tucked into their corners.

Still, this wasn't just another interview.

This wasn't a story she could collect and walk away from.

She imagined sitting across from him in his home.

Maybe not the one they had once dreamed of, but still his space.

Warm. Ordered. Unfamiliar.

Would the cushions be perfectly arranged?

Would the past sit with them like an invisible guest?

Maybe an office would be safer.

Neutral. Professional. With the distance of a desk.

Maybe the formality would protect her from herself.

But did it matter?

Whether it was a living room or a boardroom, meeting him again would open the same door.

The one she had kept closed all these years.

She would go.

Of course she would.

She had never turned down an assignment.

Because stories mattered.

Because people mattered.

But this time…

She wasn't sure if she was going as a journalist or as a woman still carrying words she had never said out loud.

The office car navigated the tree-lined avenues of an Old Delhi government colony.

Outside, the air shimmered with the late afternoon heat.

And then, the bungalow.

Grand, in a way that didn't shout.

Whitewashed walls. Wide verandas.

Power lived here, quietly.

The car slowed, then stopped.

Meera took a deep breath.

She stepped out, adjusted the strap of her bag, and walked to the gate.

She handed over her ID and letter, her face expressionless.

The guard looked at the papers, then spoke softly into his handset.

A pause.

Then, the gates opened slowly, like a curtain rising before a play that hadn't been rehearsed.

Inside, a sharply dressed assistant greeted her with mechanical warmth, leading her down a long corridor adorned with sepia photographs and antique clocks.

Time felt heavier here.

In the living room, Meera sat still.

Except for her hands, pressed tightly together in her lap.

A quiet prayer against the dull ache in her chest.

She looked around.

Too quiet.

Too still, the kind of stillness that has weight.

Her eyes drifted to the window.

Outside stood a *peepal* tree.

Old. Stubborn. Rooted.

Its leaves moved with the breeze, each rustle like a whisper.

Like memory brushing against her skin.

The peepal always found her.

She never knew why.

But there it was—again.

And in that moment, she felt it.

Not just the wind but the watching.

As if the tree remembered, even what she tried to forget.

She looked away.

It is strange how something small—a tree, a silence, a scent—can push open a door you've nailed shut.

Three years.

Since that day.

Since that silence.

Now, she would face him again.

She looked at the doorway, waiting.

And slowly, time began to slip.

She was no longer in a government bungalow.

She was at home again.

Dodging Maa's morning scoldings.

Rushing down college corridors.
Hearing his voice—how it used to stir something fierce inside her.
Back to that first glance.
When time didn't move forward.
It just paused.
Back to when it all began.

Some mornings smelled like *parathas*; others, like something unnamed.

Today, the morning smelled like change—faint but certain, like a thread pulled loose from the hem of a well-worn day.

"Meera, wake up! The tea is getting cold."

Maa's voice came sharp, slicing through the soft remnants of her sleep. Meera pulled the *dohar* closer, as if it could shield her from what awaited beyond the bed. Outside, life had already begun—utensils clattered, the temple bell chimed its morning hymn, and the newspaper landed at the door with a solid thud, the world's way of telling her to get up.

She stretched luxuriously. Her fingers brushed against the faded flowers of the bedsheet, rough like memory. The fan whirred above, pushing warm air around, not really cooling.

"Meera!" Maa's voice came again—edged now, the last warning.

Meera let out a sigh that came from somewhere deep—not tiredness exactly, but the knowledge of the beginning of another day, just like the last. Her feet met the mosaic floor—cool, chipped, ordinary. The smell of parathas reached her before she entered the kitchen, wrapping her in love dressed in *ghee*.

Maa stood over the *tava*, hands moving as they had always done.

Flip. Press. Sizzle. The sunlight broke through the half-open window in little golden spears, hitting the steel vessels and casting long, curved shadows across the floor.

"You'll never learn to run a home if you keep waking up so late," Maa said, not unkindly, placing a hot paratha in front of Meera. "When I was your age, I already knew how to prepare four dishes before sunrise."

Meera didn't argue. She tore off a piece of the paratha and dipped it into the *aloo sabzi*. The ghee kissed her fingers before melting on her tongue. For a moment, it filled something—a small ache, maybe—and then disappeared.

Between bites, Meera mumbled, "Maybe we could try something new, like bread or *samosas*?"

Maa clicked her tongue. "Bread? *Maida*? That's not food; that's fluff. And samosas? Fried nonsense. I wake up early every morning to feed this family properly, and this is what I hear?"

Out on the veranda, Baba hid behind his paper like always, thick glasses resting halfway down his nose. He smiled without looking up. This was their ritual—the push and pull between Meera and Maa, like waves crashing but never leaving the shore.

"It says here more homes are getting colour TVs," he offered casually. "Cricket in colour! Can you imagine?"

Raju perked up immediately. "Didi! *Chitrahaar* in full colour!"

And suddenly, Meera was smiling, drawn by the memory of their tiny black-and-white TV, a square miracle in their small world. Every Sunday, it turned their house into a cinema. Neighbours gathered beneath the peepal tree outside, like an audience before a stage. When *Ramayana* played on the screen, half the *mohalla* was seated on *charpais* beneath its rustling leaves.

Raju stumbled in, hair wild, his teacup sloshing.

"Maa, you forgot the sugar again. This is just disappointment in a cup."

Maa flicked his arm. "When you start earning, you can bathe in sugar. Till then, drink it as it is."

Baba laughed, setting his paper down. "Too much sugar ruins teeth. Ask your uncle. He has no teeth left—can't even bite into a *roti* now."

Raju groaned dramatically. "Why does wisdom always taste so bland?"

Baba looked at him, eyes warm. "Life isn't always sweet. It's better you learn this now."

Meera paused. Baba's words hung in the air, slow and heavy. Her friends had lives with chocolates, cousins, and foreign vacations. Hers was not like that, but it wasn't bitter either. It was stitched together with care, with effort, and with presence.

And maybe that was enough.

Raju was chaos in a uniform—books spilling, water bottle leaking, and excuses on loop.

"If you packed the night before, mornings wouldn't feel like war," Baba said gently. "Preparation is like an umbrella—no use opening it after you're soaked."

He turned to Meera, his voice quieter now.

"And remember, the early bird catches the worm."

She smirked. "Only if the bird wants a worm."

He laughed. "True. But starting early gives you options."

The morning kept rolling forward. Baba, precise as always, tied the laces of his Bata shoes, adjusted his pen, and sipped the last of his tea. At 8:30 sharp, he folded his paper and stepped outside, bag slung on his shoulder, like a soldier of routine.

Outside, the street was already full of sounds—'*aloo-tamatar-bhindi*' calls from the vendor, school kids in stiff uniforms, a cycle bell ringing from somewhere far.

Meera stood on the veranda, watching Baba walk towards the gate. The sun touched the floor, warm already. Everything was the same—the peeling walls, the morning clamour, and the unchanging flow of family life.

But inside her, something shifted.

Choices, Baba had said.

She called out, "We wake up early every day and still eat the same paratha. What choices are there?"

Baba, already at the gate, turned back and replied, "Choices aren't always on the plate; they're in how you see the plate. You can complain, or you can savour. You can call it routine, or you can find the door inside it."

She didn't answer.

The paratha still tasted like it always did. The day still looked like any other. But Baba's words had left a mark, like fingerprints on a foggy mirror—not fully visible, not yet clear, but definitely there.

Choices aren't about what's given; they're about how you receive it, with resistance or with grace.

Meera looked around the house… the familiar feel of it, the soft corners worn by time and habit. She had never really seen it before, not like this.

And just like that, something inside her stirred.

Today smelled like change.

She didn't know what it meant yet.

Only that it had arrived.

"Didi, hurry up! The rickshaw won't wait forever!"

Raju's voice sliced through the stillness like a blade of light under a closed door. It was not a call, not even a shout, but more like a small rebellion ringing through cracked walls and tin rooftops, born impatient and barefoot.

A window creaked open somewhere upstairs, probably someone murmuring a sleepy curse into the morning smog.

Meera didn't answer. She didn't need to. Some things, like Raju's yelling or Delhi's summers, didn't wait for responses. She just grabbed her bag, glancing at the mirror with a hurried glance. Her *dupatta* was a crushed afterthought, her *kajal* smudged like a half-told story.

She didn't fix it. There was no time to fix anything this morning.

The city smelled of turmeric, burnt toast, and beginnings, simmering under the kind of heat that sticks to your back like a second skin, urging you to stay wrapped in dreams and a ceiling fan's lullaby.

But Meera couldn't afford the poetry of rest. Not today.

At the gate, Kaka leaned against his rickshaw like a man in no hurry to outrun life. His turban drooped slightly to the left, like a tired sun. The rickshaw's paint was peeling, Delhi blue fading into a nostalgia-grey, but his smile held. Steady. Crooked. Familiar.

"*Namaste*, Kaka."

"Namaste, *bitiya*," he replied, his voice coarse with the dust of decades.

Raju was already there, swinging his legs.

"You're late again, Didi," he said with that wicked little grin younger brothers keep hidden behind mischief and mangoes.

"I'm not late," she muttered. "I just don't believe in racing the sun."

"The early bird catches the worm."

Meera arched an eyebrow. "Maybe the bird's tired. Maybe the worm isn't worth it today."

Kaka chuckled. With a grunt of effort, he pushed them into motion—three lives rolling forward on rusty wheels.

The streets were stories, the potholes like old arguments. The air was thick with the perfume of *puris*, citrus peels, cow dung, and *chai* leaves—all of it colliding mid-air, like memories bumping into each other in a family gathering.

They passed peeling mansions that still believed they were beautiful, temples that chimed awake, and *juicewalas* yelling prices like poets with deadlines.

And then—the protest.

Kamla Nagar had always been a canvas, but today, it bled louder.

A group of students stood near the bus stop, fists raised like commas demanding a pause in history. Their placards screamed in silence:

*Remove the Mandal Commission.*

*Say No to Reservation.*

Meera leaned forward, drawn not by agreement or curiosity but by something more primal—the same tug that makes you watch lightning before thunder.

There was a girl in the crowd. Her eyes were shining with a fierce light. She held the mic tightly. She wasn't shouting; she was asking. And somehow, that made the noise around her quieter. Something about the way she leaned in, not just to speak but also to understand, made Meera pause. It wasn't fury that lit the girl's face; it was attention.

It was as though she had made a promise to the people listening: I'm here. I care. I'll ask, even if no one answers.

Behind her, a boy raised a placard that read: *Equality is not a favour. It's a right.*

Something inside Meera flickered—not a belief, not yet, but a hunger, a need to understand where this fire was born.

Her mind drifted back to last night's dinner, its taste still heavy on her tongue. She had asked Baba, casually but curiously, "What do you think about the Mandal Commission?"

Baba had looked up from his book slowly, like truth needed a running start.

"It's a wound and a balm, Meera," he'd said, adjusting his glasses. "It's an attempt, a staircase built for those never given a door. Some call it justice, others call it unfair."

She'd nodded.

"Do protests even work?"

"Sometimes," Baba replied after a pause. "Sometimes they shake the walls, yes. But real change?"

He looked away for a moment, then back at her.

"Real change often arrives barefoot. It slips in—quiet, unnoticed—through classrooms, through courtrooms, and through conversations that don't raise their voice. Sometimes the loudest revolutions aren't shouted. They're whispered in lecture halls, at dinner tables, and in the stillness of someone finally being heard."

Now, in this moment, the echoes of that conversation wrapped around her.

Who were these children screaming at the sky?

What pain did they inherit that made them yell in public, risking comfort for conviction?

Who told them their voices mattered—and who didn't?

The rickshaw rolled on, but the questions remained.

When they reached Raju's school, he leapt off like a thought already formed.

"Don't be late, Didi. Or Baba will start with his 'youth of India' lecture again."

Meera smiled. "His lectures are better than your jokes."

Raju stuck his tongue out, his laughter bouncing off the school gate like a bell.

Now it was just her, Kaka, and the wheels.

As the sound of the protest grew fainter, its rhythm clung to her ribs—like smoke, like memory. She reached college and stepped off the rickshaw slowly.

"Bye, Kaka."

"*Khush raho,* bitiya."

She watched him pedal away, swallowed by a city that never stopped growing teeth.

The slogans had stopped ringing in her ears, but they had started whispering somewhere deeper.

Maybe tonight she'd ask Baba again.

Not about policies, but about people.

Their stories. Their scars.

Their wounds. Their waiting.

What makes someone stand on a street and yell into the wind?

What silence comes before that roar?

She wasn't ready to protest.

Not yet.

But she didn't turn away this time.

She listened.

And maybe, just maybe, that's how change begins.

Not with fists, but with ears.

Not with answers or slogans, but with questions.

As Meera stepped through the old gates of her college, the familiar morning hum wrapped around her—laughter echoing off brick walls, footsteps skipping down corridors, and heated debates rising like smoke from the cycle stand. Some students were poring over last-minute notes, brows furrowed; others waved samosas like tiny trophies, mid-argument about politics and protests.

The air smelled of chalk dust, ink, and fried oil—distractions Meera had grown fond of.

She loved samosas, not just for the golden crust and spicy aloo that burned just enough, but also because they felt like little rebellions—greasy, hot, and unapologetically eaten with fingers. At home, it was always parathas, rolled with care, served with napkins, and eaten with folded knees and folded thoughts.

Reliable. Predictable. Respectable.

But not the flaky indulgence she craved.

"One day," she thought, "I'll skip breakfast and eat a samosa right here, while it's still hot."

Some things—like change and samosas—had to be seized before they turned cold and familiar.

But today wasn't that day. Today was just another day. Or so she thought.

"Meera!"

She turned.

Pooja was racing toward her, her dupatta trailing like a flag, notes flapping under one arm.

"Where were you yesterday?" she asked, half out of breath.

"Maa sent me to the tailor with Raju," Meera said, rolling her eyes. "Apparently, I'm his secretary now."

Pooja laughed. "Your mother still thinks Raju can't cross a road without you."

"You tell her that," Meera grinned.

They walked toward class, past a group of boys loudly reenacting a cricket match with invisible balls. The walls smelled of old paper and older memories. Portraits of freedom fighters looked down from dusty frames, not judging but watching.

Inside, a small group had formed around the back bench. There was a hush, words spoken in whispers.

"What's going on?" Meera asked.

"There's a new boy," Pooja whispered. "He's joined the second year. From Kanpur. Can you believe that?"

Meera's eyes scanned the room.

He sat two rows ahead. Alone.

Medium height. Dusky skin. Hair combed neatly, but already giving in to the humidity. Full-sleeved shirt, cuffs buttoned. A pen lay perfectly parallel to his notebook—not flashy, just precise. He didn't slouch, shift, shrink, or swell like boys from smaller towns often did.

He was just there.

Not invisible. Not loud. Composed.

Like someone who didn't need the room's approval to exist in it.

Then, he looked up.

And their eyes met.

Not a glance. Not a flicker. A moment.

Still.

Curious, but not asking.

A quiet kind of noticing.

Meera's breath caught.

She was suddenly aware of the kajal smudged beneath one eye, the strands of hair that had slipped free.

She should've checked and fixed herself in the mirror. Now, under his steady gaze, all her small flaws felt oddly vivid.

He didn't look away.

He simply looked.

As if saying: I see you. And it's enough.

She turned, cheeks warm, heart not racing but stirring.

The room felt quieter, as if everything had paused to let that second breathe.

Then Professor Iyer entered, with his usual stack of handouts and sharp glare that could hush a thunderstorm.

"Settle down," he said, scanning the class.

His eyes landed on the second row.

"This is Aman Verma," he said. "From Kanpur. Joined mid-session. Top marks. Let's make him feel welcome."

Aman nodded. A few mumbled greetings followed.

Meera tried to focus, but the name—Aman—clung to her mind like chalk dust on fingers.

A plain name. An everyday name.

And yet, it had already begun to take up space in her thoughts.

"We didn't even speak," she thought. "Just one look. That's all. And still…"

The lecture turned to post-independence India.

Her attention wandered.

A voice from the back of the classroom asked, “Sir, what’s your opinion on the Mandal Commission protests?”

A ripple. Murmurs spread.

“My brother missed his exam.”

“They might shut down the library,” someone whispered.

“Good. In fact, let it burn. Maybe someone will listen.”

Professor Iyer raised a hand. “Enough. We’ll discuss this during the seminar. I expect all of you to come prepared, for and against. You’ll all speak.”

The room fell quiet again, not calm, just quieter.

After class was over, bags rustled, and debates resumed.

Meera found herself walking behind Aman, just close enough to hear his voice.

“I don’t think protests are meaningless,” he said, in a calm and measured tone. “But shouting isn’t the only way to be heard.”

The boy beside him scoffed. “Then what? Sit at home and hope?”

Aman looked at him, not offended or shaken.

“Not all change needs a megaphone,” he replied. “Some of us want to change things from the inside.”

“And how do you plan to do that?” the boy asked.

Aman’s voice was soft but unwavering. “By getting to where decisions are made. And not forgetting why I wanted to be there in the first place.”

No slogans. No fire. Just a quiet certainty.

Meera felt something stir within her.

It wasn’t an attraction in the usual way.

Not movie-scene romance. Not the stuff you write in journals.

He wasn’t beautiful; he was anchored.

Like someone who knew the ground he stood on.

And for a moment, she wanted to stand beside him.

The next professor arrived. Students shuffled back to their seats.

Aman looked up. Their eyes met again, just briefly.

No smile. No nod. Just a flicker of shared stillness.

Like two people catching the same shift in the wind.

Not a storm.

Not a revolution.

Just a hush.

The kind that slips in unnoticed, like sunlight warming a corner no one looks at.

Some changes don't shake the world.

They don't echo through streets or make front-page headlines.

Some changes only stir inside you—a breath held, a thought unspoken, or a glance that lingers longer than it should.

No one else noticed.

But she did.

And she knew something had begun.

Not a love story. Not yet.

But the scent of one, like rain in the air before it falls.

Because not all revolutions are loud.

Some begin in silence.

And the heart, without warning, learns a new rhythm.

The peepal tree outside the classroom had stood there forever, its leaves whispering secrets no one else could hear. It had watched friendships bloom and wither, caught stolen glances between pages and laughter tangled with nervous words.

Today, it listened to a heart beating a little louder than before—Meera's.

She should have been following the lecture, but her pen spun between her fingers, her mind drifting to the new boy, Aman.

It was not love at first sight. She didn't believe in that fairy tale.

Movies made it look easy—one look, one moment, and the rest written in the stars.

But real life was different—missed chances, awkward silences, and feelings that slipped away before they could mean anything.

Still, something had shifted the moment Aman's eyes met hers.

"Are you taking notes or writing a love story in your head?" Pooja whispered, smirking.

Meera blinked at her blank notebook. Ten minutes lost.

"My pen stopped working," she muttered, scrambling for words as the professor moved on.

Pooja laughed softly. "Or maybe your brain did."

Meera glared at her. "Just shut up."

Outside, life carried on—footsteps echoing in the corridor,

laughter spilling from windows, and distant rickshaw horns weaving through the afternoon.

Usually, she'd be out there too, skipping lectures and wandering the lanes of Kamla Nagar with Pooja.

"Let's go for some ice cream and window shopping. We'll be back before the next class," Pooja coaxed, eyes sparkling with mischief.

Meera hesitated. She would normally agree, but today…

"You go ahead. I'll come later."

Pooja raised an eyebrow. "Since when do you skip Kamla Nagar?"

Meera shrugged, avoiding her gaze. She was not ready to admit why she lingered near the door.

Aman slung his bag over his shoulder and paused by her side.

"Uh… Meera, right?"

Her breath caught, not because he knew her name—everyone did—but because he said it.

"Yes," she nodded, fingers fiddling with her bangles.

"Where's the library?"

She blinked. "You mean… the place with all the books?"

He chuckled. "Yes, that one."

She wanted to disappear, not because of him but because of how ridiculous she sounded. It was as though she'd just described a secret realm from a storybook.

Pooja watched from the corner, a smile tugging at her lips.

Meera cleared her throat. "Go straight down the corridor, then turn right."

Aman nodded. "Thanks." And he was gone.

Three seconds later, Pooja burst out laughing.

"The place with all the books? Smooth, Meera!"

Meera groaned, closing her notebook.

"Now that Mr Library's gone, do you want to come to Kamla Nagar?"

Pooja wiggled her eyebrows and added, "I promise I won't tease you. Much."

Meera rolled her eyes but said nothing.

Her gaze drifted back to the peepal tree, its leaves stirring in the warm breeze, whispering stories of moments like these.

She exhaled slowly.

"I think I'll stay."

Pooja held up her hands. "Suit yourself. Just don't sit here daydreaming about —"

Meera shot her a look.

"Fine, fine," Pooja laughed, walking away.

Alone, Meera leaned against the door frame, feeling a flutter inside.

Was this the start of something?

She didn't know yet.

But under the peepal tree's quiet rustle, it felt like the first breath of a story waiting to be told.

It began with something as ordinary as a wooden chair, worn smooth by years of shifting bodies and restless hands. It was wobbly, with one leg shorter than the rest, etched over time with names, doodles, and forgotten equations. But it was his, in the second row, third from the left, never marked, never claimed, yet somehow his. Until the day it wasn't.

Meera remembered it with the kind of clarity reserved for things that don't seem important—until they are. She was already seated with Pooja, absently flipping through her notes, when Aman walked in. He paused briefly near his usual spot, but someone else had occupied it. It was a boy from another group, mid-laugh, sitting with his legs sprawled, completely unaware of the quiet claim he had trespassed.

Aman said nothing. Not a word. Not a frown. Just a pause, like a comma in an unfinished sentence. Then, with no sign of protest, he turned and scanned the room for another seat. Pooja, always at ease with other people's moments, patted the space beside her.

"Come on, Aman. This one's free."

For a second, Meera thought he'd walk away and choose a corner, an edge, or some seat that asked nothing of him.

But then, he sat down, right there, beside her.

It was a moment so small it might have gone unnoticed, but something in the air changed. A stillness threaded through the noise.

At first, Aman barely spoke. Pooja filled the gaps, flitting from gossip to grievances. Meera spoke too, but less freely. With Aman beside her, she noticed the silence more, not as absence but as presence—weighty and full.

Aman's words were like punctuation—precise, never wasted.

Maybe that's what drew her in.

Pooja, of course, had no patience for care.

"Why are you always so serious?" she asked one afternoon, as they waited under the peepal tree, books balanced on knees, the sun slicing through leaves.

Aman looked up, not defensive, just amused. "I don't talk simply to fill silence."

Pooja groaned dramatically. "They call this boring, you know? I'm sure you've heard the term."

Meera smiled, a retort forming before she even knew it was hers. And then, like a truth too heavy to hold, it slipped out.

"Aman's not boring," she said. "Honestly, I could sit with him forever and not feel the time pass."

It landed too fast, like a secret blurted under one's breath.

The pause afterwards stretched just a little too long.

Meera's cheeks flamed. The sentence had tumbled out with such certainty, and she hadn't realized how much it would reveal. Pooja raised an eyebrow in half-mockery, half-surprise.

"Really? Forever?" she said, her voice teasing.

Aman didn't laugh or flinch. He simply looked at Meera, like he was turning the sentence over in his mind. Not judging. Just… noticing.

Meera, suddenly unsure of what to do with her hands, her voice, and her face, stood up too quickly.

"I need water," she blurted.

"Now?" Pooja asked, puzzled.

"Yes. Now."

Meera left before they could respond, walking fast, as though she could outpace her own words. But she could still feel them behind her in the silence she left and in Aman's eyes. With most people, silence begged to be filled, but with Aman, it never felt awkward; it felt like a language on its own.

She wanted to tell him so, but didn't.

Not then.

After that day, Aman didn't sit with them again for a while. There was no explanation or awkward exchange, just a quiet retreat to his old seat.

Everything looked the same, but something had changed.

Meera didn't know if she missed him or if she just noticed his absence more than she expected to.

The days passed by. Classes came and went. The group projects, chai breaks, and last-minute submissions continued as usual. Some things faded, like chalk on a board not fully erased, but the tea break stayed on—Meera and Pooja, two cups of tea, sun-warmed benches, and a hundred conversations spilling over plastic tables.

Aman was never part of this clutter. He moved through the day like a soft wind, books hugged to his chest, always somewhere else.

Until the afternoon, he wasn't.

She saw him at the canteen door, his eyes scanning, not searching. He spotted her.

Their eyes met—not for long, just a glance.

He walked in and ordered tea. He held it in both hands like warmth itself. Then, without fanfare, he pulled out a chair and sat across from them.

Like he'd always been there.

Like nothing had happened.

Pooja barely noticed, but Meera did.

He didn't speak. He didn't need to. He was just… there. Listening. Sitting. Allowing the noise in the canteen to pass through him like wind through trees.

Meera watched him covertly and wondered.

Could the three of them last? Could a spark, a breeze, and a tide really hold each other?

She didn't know, but she wanted to believe it.

She liked to believe she was a little of both—Pooja's fire and Aman's stillness. Maybe that's why it worked, a triangle that balanced itself, not by symmetry, but by silence.

And somewhere, quietly, a wish formed.

Her father used to say, "When you wish, do so clearly. The universe is always listening."

She hadn't realized it then, but that day, she wished for this strange, steady rhythm between the three of them to last.

Time moved differently after that. No big changes. No announcements. Just a slow tilt.

Some days, Aman would sit with them; on others, he wouldn't. But when he did, it felt easy, like an answer, not a question.

Until one afternoon, the balance shifted.

Pooja had to leave early.

For the first time, it was just Meera and Aman.

She braced for awkwardness, but it didn't come.

The silence between them was different. Clean. Honest. Like shared breath under the shade of a tree.

After a while, she turned to him.

"That day… when Pooja called you boring," she said softly, "I didn't mean it like that. I meant… silence isn't boring. Not always."

Aman didn't rush to reply. He let a leaf fall from between his fingers, then looked up.

"I know what you meant."

A pause.

"Silence, with the right people, is company," he said. "And you… You're the right kind of person for someone like me, a boring person." It wasn't a confession. Not exactly.

But it lingered.

Not between them but within her.

And somehow, it spoke louder than anything he'd ever said.

She didn't name it.

She didn't need to.

If the canteen was their afternoon refuge, the library was Aman's sanctuary.

Unlike most students who only drifted in during exams, Aman treated the library like a second home. He had a quiet spot tucked near the back, by the old peepal tree outside the window. It wasn't just about reading—he needed the silence. He didn't just borrow books; he stayed with them.

He never asked anyone to join him. He'd simply say, "I'll be in the library," like an open door—not a request, not a plea—just there, waiting.

She told herself not to overthink it. Maybe that was just how he was—quiet, reserved. Still, a part of her wished that he'd looked her in the eye, just once, and said, "Come."

And yet, she began to show up in the library. More often than necessary.

She'd sit a few tables away, flipping through notes she didn't need, highlighting lines just to look busy. She wasn't sure what she was waiting for—maybe nothing. Maybe everything.

The only thing in her way was Pooja.

If it weren't for Pooja, she'd have spent all her time there. But Pooja couldn't stand libraries. If she had even tried to enjoy sitting in the library, Meera would've gladly spent all her spare moments there. But the moment she mentioned it, Pooja would groan in protest.

"Books and silence? That's not college life! Meera, please! It smells like dust and despair in there. We're young! This is our time to live—to do something fun, not get lost in piles of books."

Meera hadn't always loved them either.

Most days, she accompanied Pooja wherever she went. She let Pooja drag her to Kamla Nagar, where laughter fizzed louder than the soda, trying not to think about Aman and wondering if he noticed when she wasn't there.

But on some days, when she could slip away unnoticed, she found herself sitting near that quiet corner, pretending to study, sneaking glances at how he tapped his pen absentmindedly, and flipping through books she didn't need to read.

At first, she reached for textbooks—reference guides—pretending to be absorbed in course material. But over time, when that pretence grew heavy, she started reaching for novels instead. She'd always loved stories, sometimes even non-fiction, but had never let herself choose them freely before.

When Aman once noticed, he said, "Don't be afraid to pick what you enjoy reading. It should be your choice, not anyone else's."

That stayed with her.

It wasn't about the books; it was about choosing what felt right. It was about letting something matter, not because it made sense, but because it was her choice.

It wasn't borrowed. It was hers.

Slowly, she began to wonder if she could make her choice clear to him, too. Could she, one day, sit beside him with no book at all, no excuse, no need to explain?

Just be there.

Because, like the novels she now read without guilt, Aman, too, wasn't an obligation. He was a choice—one she wasn't ready to say out loud yet, but one she'd already made in her quiet, certain way.

On days when Aman was in the library and she wasn't, Meera would sit with Pooja under the peepal tree. She always chose the bench facing the tall windows, right where she knew Aman usually sat. She couldn't see him. She didn't know if he looked up. But she looked anyway.

She felt close to him.

It was strange—this quiet connection. Unnamed. Unexplained. Like a thread stretched between them, invisible but unmistakably there.

She didn't know what it was.

Infatuation? A passing thing?

Or something slower, quieter, gathering in the background before she even gave it a name?

There was a tug of war inside her.

Between the girl who always went where Pooja went—carefree, agreeable, effortlessly swept into her orbit—and the girl drawn toward the calm of Aman's presence, steady and silent.

To stay where things were loud and certain or to follow a feeling she wasn't ready to define aloud.

Pooja, of course, had noticed. She wasn't the kind to miss things like that.

Now and then, she'd nudge Meera with a grin.

"Someone's turning into a bookworm. Or maybe… It's not the books she's after, but a certain bookworm who practically lives in the library."

Meera would laugh and roll her eyes, hoping to hide everything she wasn't ready to admit—not even to herself.

Luckily, Pooja got distracted easily. A squirrel, a stumbling professor, the *chaiwala* arguing with the mess staff—anything would do.

Even if Pooja suspected something, she couldn't be sure.

How could she be sure when even Meera didn't know what it was?

Meera had never believed in instant love—and this wasn't that.

But something had shifted the day he first walked into their classroom.

Aman, with his quietness, didn't ask for attention.

Not shy, just still.

The kind of stillness that felt full, not hollow.

He didn't try to make friends.

He didn't turn on charm like the others.

He only spoke words he meant, words chosen like stones for skipping—deliberate, few, and smooth on the surface.

That's what stayed with her.

Not his face. Not his clothes.

But the calm around him.

The way silence seemed to follow him, not as a shadow, but as something he'd made peace with.

She hadn't fallen for him.

It was slower than that.

Like realizing you've been holding your breath around everyone else, and then, without meaning to, you start breathing again because someone made space for it. It wasn't love.

Not yet.

But something had begun. Quiet. Certain. Less like a seed planted, more like a rhythm found. Something that had always been there, waiting for her to notice.

It was slower, gentler.

Like rain on a quiet afternoon.

Like a song you don't notice at first, but later realize you've been humming all day.

It crept in through small moments—the way he sat, the way he listened, the way his silences said more than words ever could.

It wasn't the kind of love that shouted.

It was the kind that stayed.

A quiet flame.

It was not flashy, but constant.

Steady.

It was not something that bloomed in a rush, but something that waited, something that held space, quietly, until she was ready to call it by its name.

It had been three days since Aman had last come to the campus, and his absence hung in the air like the echo of a name half-remembered. The third day felt like a fever dream cooling in a cracked teacup. Time, already strange on campus, slowed, stretching thin like sugar pulled too far, too fast, into glass threads.

His absence didn't shout; it whispered. In the vacant seat. In the half smile that never arrived. In the silence that gathered where his laughter used to live.

Meera noticed his absence the way seasons change—not in the sky, but in the body. A heaviness in the bones. A stillness in the breath.

She found Pooja in the girls' common room, sprawled across the floor with a book in hand.

"Have you noticed?" Meera asked softly, her voice trying not to fold under its own weight. "Aman hasn't been coming to class for three days."

But worry is never subtle. It seeps through pauses and unspoken names.

Pooja didn't look up. Her reply came like a shrug stitched with sarcasm. "He's probably memorizing the Constitution. He'll resurface once he hits Article 395."

Meera didn't say anything but just gave her a look, the kind that held both impatience and quiet ache, like a thread pulled too tight.

Then, as if the air had shifted, Pooja closed the book with a thud that sounded too loud in the quiet and sat up, brushing imaginary dust from her lap.

"Well," she said, rising, "if he's hiding in the library behind a stack of books like some tragic philosopher, I swear I'm going to mix up all his notes as punishment."

They checked the library first, not because they thought he would be there, but because they needed to believe he might be. The rustle of pages, the low hum of fluorescent lights—everything was the same except him.

His chair was still warm in memory but cold in truth.

They looked for him at the bench under the peepal tree where he sometimes scribbled lines of poetry during study breaks. He wasn't there. They searched the back corner of the canteen where he dissected political theory over lukewarm chai. Empty.

That's the thing with absence—it makes the ordinary unbearable.

They took a rickshaw. The ride was jerky, uneven, but familiar like most things in college—chaotic but coded in comfort. The roads coughed dust. The wind smelt of samosas and lost time.

They reached his hostel. The building stood like a tired book—spine cracked, windows blinking sleep.

Meera knocked once, twice, a third time, as if calling someone back from a dream.

When the door opened, the air inside moved differently—slower, heavier, like it had been mourning.

Aman stood there, leaning against the frame like someone trying not to fall. His eyes were moons drained of light, his body, a frayed syllabus of willpower and neglect.

"You idiot," Pooja said, but it sounded like "we missed you".

The room was a story in contrast to him.

Where Aman looked unravelled, the room was rigid with order.

It was as if he had poured every last bit of control into its corners and left only the disarray for himself.

The bed was made with military precision, the pillow aligned like it awaited inspection.

His desk stood like a shrine to discipline—books stacked in silent towers, spines staring back, notes pinned to the wall like prayers.

A single glass of water sat untouched, as if even thirst had learned to wait.

One sticky note in capital letters: IAS.

No punctuation. No hesitation. Only obsession.

Meera stared at it.

He wasn't just preparing for the exam.

He was dissolving into it.

"I had a fever. Just mild. I'm okay now," he said, as if okay was a language he'd been forced to learn.

But sickness leaves a trace—the hollow behind the cheekbones, the silence in the eyes. Meera saw it. All of it.

She didn't reach for him. She didn't ask why he didn't call. She just watched.

Because sometimes watching is the closest we get to loving.

Pooja, unable to remain still, crashed into the chair like she was trying to shake the silence out of the room.

"You look like a ghost that passed the prelims," she said, tossing a cushion at him.

Aman smiled, but only with his mouth. His eyes stayed behind.

There were empty strips of medicine on the desk. A towel was dried. A copy of *The Hindu*, unread.

"Why didn't you tell us?" Meera finally asked. Her voice was not angry. Not even hurt. Just… soft. Like a leaf brushing a window.

He looked away.

"There was no way to tell you," he said.

This was both true and untrue, like most things in their lives.

Back then, there was no WhatsApp, no blue ticks to haunt you. If you vanished, you vanished.

But the body knows. The body of a friend knows when something's wrong.

Outside, a dog barked at nothing. A crow called but was not answered.

Meera turned toward the door, then paused and looked back. His eyes met hers, and something unnamed passed between them—a thread, a tremor.

The kind of moment that doesn't belong to love yet but no longer belongs to friendship.

She wanted to tell him, "You don't always have to do this alone."

She wanted to tell him, "Your strength is beautiful, but your softness is not a sin."

Instead, she said, "Get some rest."

Which is how we say "I care" when the world has not given us permission to do so.

And then she left, carrying his absence with her, not as a wound, but as a whisper.

After she left, Aman sat on the edge of his perfectly made bed, in a room that had not changed, except now it held a little more warmth.

Meera glanced back once at the faint glow from Aman's window. Something stirred within her—a tangle of worry, helplessness, and something softer, something she wasn't ready to name yet.

That was the first and last time she ever saw Aman's room.

At least, the one in Delhi.

It had been exactly eighteen months and twelve days since Meera and Pooja first met Aman.

It had been eighteen months and twelve days since Aman entered their orbit—Meera counting, Pooja forgetting, and Aman unaware.

In that time, a thousand things had changed. Semester schedules. Friendships like shifting tectonic plates. The taste of coffee in the mess.

But one thing didn't—Aman's plan.

It was not just a goal you pin to your pillow or whisper into late-night calls. His plan was a living thing, alive in the margins of notebooks, in the hum of his breath as he studied, in the way he looked past the classroom windows like he was already somewhere else.

IAS.

Three letters, heavy like a father's expectation, like history stitched into his surname.

It wasn't just ambition; it was grammar.

He spoke in timelines. In optional subjects. In phases: Prelims, Mains, Interview.

While the rest of them flirted with deadlines and each other, Aman moved like someone who already knew the ending of the story.

It wasn't arrogance; it was belief.

"I'll stay here for my master's," he said once, like it was nothing. Like he hadn't just declared war on fate and chosen his own battlefield.

He meant Delhi University. He meant staying close to the dream.

He meant: "I will not leave what I've built."

But life isn't a schedule. It doesn't care for discipline, dreams, or quiet boys in well-ironed shirts.

One morning, the call came.

It was not the result he'd waited for. This brought an ending.

His father's heart gave up.

Just stopped.

Like someone switching off the light mid-sentence.

The next day, Aman was no longer a student. He was a son. A provider. A man.

Kanpur called him back with a voice louder than any ambition.

His mother didn't cry in public. His sister clutched his arm like a question she was afraid to ask.

And Aman folded his dreams the way you fold an old letter—neatly, slowly, with both hands, as if it were made of glass.

An uncle offered him a job in Bangalore. Safe. Sensible. A salary that arrived with the calendar. Predictable. Painless.

It wasn't a life; it was a compromise wearing a suit.

But what is duty if not a love too heavy to carry?

So, he returned to Delhi one last time, not as a student, not as the boy with the plan.

He packed his books like farewell letters, buttoned his shirts with the precision of grief.

No farewell party. No speeches. Just silence.

Meera stood at the gate, her eyes asking questions her mouth never learned to shape.

Pooja smiled, the kind that forgives what words cannot hold.

Aman didn't say much. He never had to.

His silences always said more than sentences could.

Then, almost like an afterthought, or maybe a confession, he looked at them and said quietly, "I have only one regret—that life did not let me choose." But grief doesn't wait. It doesn't pause for the right time. Life moves on, whether we're ready or not. Aman had no choice but to move with it. He left quickly, carrying burdens heavier than his bags.

And then, he was gone.

No dramatic exits. No looking back.

Delhi slipped away, just like Aman's dream, fading quietly despite the months of studying, endless chai, and midnight hopes. It was a city he had memorized with his footsteps. Kanpur was only a pause, long enough to be remembered, short enough to leave without breaking anything. He didn't go with anger or carry regret. Just that soft ache of someone who had once hoped. And now hoped elsewhere.

Bangalore didn't open its arms to him. It folded him in like a file, tucked neatly into a drawer called responsibility. The world that had once stretched wide with possibility now narrowed down to a checklist, bills, and alarm clocks. He took small steps and began again.

Pooja arrived in the same city like rain in a drought. Her move was unexpected but exactly what she needed. Her world opened like the sky after a storm: wide, blue, full of things still to come. She didn't map her way in; she moved with the wind, with instinct. With timing. With a little help from chance.

Her sister cracked the door open with a job in the media—entry-level, hardly a title. Her brother-in-law was already in that world, a journalist in Bangalore. And through that sliver of chance, something opened. For Pooja, it was enough. Headlines and deadlines. Stories waiting in silence. While Aman moved like a man counting his steps, she moved like breath, unplanned, but full of direction.

And just like that, Aman and Pooja found themselves in the same city.

Far from Meera. And even farther from who they once were.

Meera stayed. Not because she had to, but because nothing called her away.

She didn't apply anywhere, didn't pack or plan. She stayed like silence does—in the corners, in the folds of routine, hoping clarity would find her.

Aman had a duty. Pooja had direction.

Meera had questions she hadn't learned how to shape into words.

Though Pooja and Aman now shared a city, their orbits never touched.

Pooja vanished into the newsroom hours—headlines, caffeine, the electric hum of stories trying to be born.

Aman, too, was finding his way in the new job.

But it wasn't the work that kept him distant. It was the hush.

A quiet kind of turning inward, like a door slowly closing from the inside.

Not from pressure, but from something softer—disinterest.

Like light fading, not because it must, but because it can.

In the early weeks, he sent letters to Meera.

Not love letters, just polite echoes. Weather reports. Work updates.

The kind of words you send when you don't know what to say but still want to be heard.

But soon, most of those stopped.

And the few that did arrive read like envelopes carrying no air—no stories, no questions, no fingerprints of the boy who once laughed with his whole body.

Only lines written with the precision of someone folding paper, not feeling.

He never called, not because she had asked him not to, not even because he didn't want to, but because he knew.

In homes like hers, middle-class and quiet with their rules, a call from a boy, who was neither kin nor fiancé, could ring louder than it should. It could echo in hallways, glances, and closed-door whispers.

So, he gave her what the world would not: silence.

Not absence. Not neglect. Just silence—the only form of respect that didn't need an explanation.

And it wasn't new. Even back in college, he had never called. Not once. Because sometimes, even the gentlest friendships weren't allowed to unfold.

So, he never said it. And she never expected it.

They had learned how to stay close without crossing lines. Theirs was a closeness built in shadows—notes passed, smiles caught mid-corridor, long walks with short conversations. Love, maybe. But shaped to fit within the silence they were born into.

Pooja called often, her voice a familiar shape in the air, soft and warm, folding over Meera like an old shawl. Pooja spoke of the usual things—how the new manager kept using words like "synergy", how someone in accounts spilled coffee on a printer, how she missed Delhi winters. Little things, the kind that stitch a day together without asking to be remembered.

And when Aman came up—as he sometimes did—her voice didn't change. "He's fine," Pooja would say, like brushing lint off a sleeve, and move on.

Just that. Nothing more.

Like a door gently closed before you can see the room inside.

And Meera, knowing better, never knocked. Never asked.

There are silences you grow used to.

Silences that hum like old refrigerators, always there but no longer heard.

Then, Aman stopped writing.

And even in the noise of daily life—buses, emails, endless laundry—something shifted. A change in Pooja's tone. A stutter in her rhythm.

Grief, Meera thought, sometimes speaks in hesitations.

That night, with the ceiling fan spinning above like a slow thought, she finally asked Pooja, "And Aman… how is he?"

There was a pause, not just of seconds but of understanding rearranging itself.

"He's… different," Pooja said, each syllable placed gently, like stepping barefoot across broken glass.

"Different how?" Meera asked, sitting up, suddenly upright inside her own fear.

"He's drowning in work. Not just long hours but deep hours. The kind that hollows you out from the inside. He doesn't talk much and eats like it's a task. I watch him, and he's there, but something in him isn't."

She paused again, and when she spoke, her voice was almost an echo.

"It's like he's fading."

The words landed like snow, quiet but changing everything they touched.

Fading.

A word like smoke, visible, then not. Felt, then gone.

Meera repeated it, not to ask but to hold it.

"He's walking in a loop," she said. "He wasn't made for this life."

"Not like this," said Pooja. "This city, this job is a cage with glass walls. You can see out, but you can't leave. He used to dream out loud, remember? Now he barely dreams at all. He's moving, but not forward. Just… in circles. Like someone erased the map and left him with nothing but the ground."

Meera heard the quiet, unravelling ache in Pooja's voice.

Like something breaking, gently.

Like a bird forgetting how to land.

So, she didn't speak or fill the silence.

Because some silences are not absences.

They're invitations.

And in that long stillness between two friends, Meera finally understood:

Aman wasn't gone. Not yet.

But he was leaving.

And no one was holding the hem of his sleeve. No one was whispering, "Stay."

A heavy silence settled like dust.

And then, something in Pooja's words, a single, quiet sentence, dropped into that silence, shook loose a memory. One that had been tucked away, forgotten like a jacket left behind in another season.

It had been a late evening at home, soft light puddling in corners, books lounging open across the bed like tired companions. They had been studying side by side, as they often did. Pooja, with her usual, impossible balance of stillness and spark, switched between debates on justice and laughter, as if it were the same language.

She noticed things. Not the things written on paper, but the ones trembling just beneath the skin.

That night, Meera had said Aman's name again. She hadn't even noticed how many times it had passed through her lips, like a prayer she didn't mean to say out loud.

Pooja looked up, her smile a curve, both knowing and kind. There was a flicker in her eyes, like she'd caught something Meera didn't even know she'd dropped.

"You talk about him a lot, you know," she said.

Tap, tap. Her pen against the page. A rhythm of quiet truths.

Meera rolled her eyes, quick with deflection. "He's a friend. That's all."

But Pooja shut her book like an answer and leaned back, her arms behind her head, relaxed in the way only someone deeply sure of what they saw could be.

"Mmm-hmm," she hummed, dragging the sound just long enough to pull a thread loose inside Meera's chest.

A cushion flew, laughter chasing it like children in the dark.

Pooja caught it mid-air, her laugh as bright as glass in sunlight.

"If I had a rupee for every time you said his name, I'd be rich by now."

Meera scoffed and brushed it off. But her cheeks betrayed her with a blush blooming like something half-remembered.

"You're being ridiculous," she said, but even her voice sounded uncertain, like it was reaching for a different script.

The laughter stilled.

Something softer fell between them.

Pooja's gaze lingered, no longer teasing. Just quiet. Just real.

"Am I?" she asked, and the words landed gently, like rain on tired skin.

Meera looked away, pretending to read. But the letters on the page had dissolved, leaving only white space and the roar of a truth she wasn't ready to accept.

Then, Pooja asked softly, "Meera, have you ever thought about it?"

Meera's breath paused.

"Thought about what?"

Pooja tilted her head, the way one does when listening not just with ears but with memory. She didn't answer. Just waited and gave Meera the silence to fill herself.

And in that waiting, something broke open.

Not loudly. Not with drama. But like petals unfolding toward a truth they'd always known.

It wasn't just friendship. It had never been.

There had always been too much of him in her. The way he spoke, the words he chose. The silence he left behind. She had carried him like a soft ache. A quiet gravity.

And now, here, in this moment, with Pooja watching her like someone who had already read the ending, Meera saw it.

Clearly.

Finally.

She didn't say a word, and Pooja didn't ask her to.

This was their friendship: soft, unhurried, fluent in pauses. In the languages between words.

After that night, something in their silences changed. They held more.

More honesty.

More tenderness.

More of the things Meera couldn't yet speak of but knew Pooja had already heard.

It was the first time Meera allowed herself to know what had always been true.

Not in sentences.

Not in declarations.

But in stillness.

At a glance.

In the way love sometimes arrives, quietly, but never unnoticed.

A confession, not to the world, just to herself.

And to Pooja.

A love not yet spoken, but deeply known.

After Aman left—and Pooja, too—Meera tried to suppress everything, as if feelings were dust and she, a broom.

She told herself these were just memories. Just names in old sentences. That she was fine, that love had an off switch.

But now, holding the phone to her ear, with Pooja's voice trembling like a thread pulled too tight, the memory came rushing in, bright, uninvited.

And with it came the ache she had trained herself to silence.

It had never just been concern, not with Aman.

She remembered the way his silences wrapped around her, a language made of absence, how the world shifted slightly off-axis when he wasn't near.

She had learned to mistranslate the feeling, file it under friendship, and stack it neatly in the corner of her mind.

But some things resist neatness.

Some truths wait like seeds under snow.

Now, with Aman slipping into a life that dimmed him, something inside Meera cracked, the kind of quiet fracture that doesn't make a sound but changes everything.

The truth was no longer whispering. It was standing in the room.

"Meera, are you there?"

Pooja's voice pulled her back. Meera blinked. Her throat tightened.

"Why didn't you ever tell me?" she asked, the hurt tucked behind her words like a shadow.

"I didn't know what to say," Pooja said softly. "I didn't know what you could do, except worry. But now I'm telling you because maybe you don't just have to worry. Maybe you get to do something."

A pause. Then Pooja added, brighter now, "There's an opening at my office. I have already recommended you."

"What?" Meera asked. "Me? But I don't even have a journalism degree."

"So?" Pooja laughed easily, like wind lifting a curtain. "Neither do I. It's not about paper. It's about voice. And heart. You have both."

Meera said nothing because Pooja wasn't wrong.

"Maybe you didn't have some big, burning dream. But this isn't it, Meera. Doing nothing was never your plan."

And in that silence, something shifted.

Not because of Aman.

Not only.

The truth was she'd been lost.

Since college ended, the days had melted together, quiet and formless. She floated through hours like a ghost in her own life, scrolling through fragments of a self she didn't know how to gather.

She told herself it was rest. But rest isn't this heavy or hollow.

She hadn't told anyone how strange it felt to wake up without reason, to move without motion, to be surrounded by noise and still feel erased.

And now, this offer, this pull toward Bangalore. Toward Aman.

A part of her wanted to see him, to know what had faded in him.

But more than that, she longed for the days when she felt, when laughter wasn't rare, when belonging didn't feel borrowed.

She missed Pooja's noise, Aman's quiet, the way she used to matter in rooms that held both. But beneath it all was a deeper longing.

Not to chase love.

But to become someone she could love.

To be needed not for her concern, but for her worth.

To step out of the in between and claim something—anything—as her own.

Maybe the interview wasn't a job. Maybe it was a doorway.

"Alright," she said slowly. "I'll come."

On the other end, Pooja smiled into the silence. "I knew you would. Meera, this is your moment."

The line held the weight of something new.

Possibility.

A life not yet lived, humming faintly under her skin.

Pooja's voice turned tender again.

"Aman needs you, Meera. But don't forget, you do, too. You need you."

Meera closed her eyes and let the words fall.

Yes, it was about Aman.

Yes, it was about her.

For too long, she had waited at the edge of her own life, watching, not stepping in.

Maybe it was time.

She took a breath, steady and full.

Maybe this was the change she hadn't known she was waiting for.

Maybe it wasn't just about going.

Maybe it was about finally arriving within herself.

She looked out the window, the sky folding into dusk, the air holding its breath like she was.

Yes, she was scared. Yes, Aman still mattered.

But so did she.

And maybe, for the first time in a long while, that was enough.

The day had stirred something inside her, quiet, certain, almost defiant. But it was the night that gave it shape.

That night, the air at dinner felt heavier than the food on their plates.

Meera sat straighter than usual, as if her spine knew this was not a meal but a moment.

"There's an interview," she said, trying to sound casual. "In Bangalore. I want to go."

Maa's frown arrived before her words did. "If you want to work, find something here in Delhi. Why vanish into a strange city?"

Baba didn't speak. He rarely did in the beginning and let things unfold.

Meera steadied her breath. "I don't have experience. Pooja's already spoken to someone there. If I don't make it, I'll come back. Just give me a week."

"A week?" Maa shook her head in disbelief. "Why chase something you're not even trained for? Girls your age should be thinking about settling down, not chasing jobs in strange cities."

Meera's fingers curled around the edge of the table. Her voice, when it came, was sharper than she intended.

"Then I'm not qualified for marriage either."

Maa blinked.

"I don't know how to cook as you do. I'm messy. I forget to put lids back on jars. So should I stay home and train for that instead?"

The words dropped like stones into silence. Baba kept chewing, but Meera knew he had heard everything.

In the quiet, his voice from long ago echoed in her mind:

"Words are arrows. Once released, you can't call them back. But your tone—that can still dress the wound."

He had taught her diplomacy, not defeat. That grace had its own kind of power.

She loosened her grip and softened her gaze.

"Let me try, Maa. Just once. I'm not asking forever."

Maa turned to Baba, her eyes full of expectation.

Baba, steady as ever, put down his spoon. His voice was calm, but it cut through everything else.

"Let her try. Birds don't perch on the same branch forever. She should have the sky to choose from."

That was it.

Baba's "yes" was never loud, but it always unlocked the door. Maa might circle back later, but for now, this was done.

Meera nodded, gratitude heavy on her tongue.

But something in her paused.

Yes, Baba had allowed it.

But why did it need permission?

Even in his kindness, the truth pricked—this, too, was patriarchy.

Just softer. Polished. Loving.

Wrapped in fatherly affection, but still in the same cage.

Her freedom had arrived dressed as a favour.

She didn't want a life like that.

She didn't want a husband she had to convince.

She didn't want to be handed permission like a child asking

for sweets.

She wanted a partnership.

A seat at the table, not beneath it.

A life built on shared decisions, not inherited silence.

And in that flicker of fury and clarity, the truth finally burned through:

She wasn't going only for Aman.

She wasn't just following old laughter or unfinished feelings.

She was stepping toward herself.

Toward space. Breath. Becoming.

This wasn't just a job.

It was an opening in the wall.

A passage out of a quiet life where she'd faded into the wallpaper.

She wasn't running toward love.

She was running toward liberation.

In a middle-class Indian home, a girl who isn't studying or working is considered a ticking clock.

And that clock was winding down.

Maa had begun preparing. Quietly.

The train called marriage had begun pulling onto the platform.

Rekha *Bua* had already stepped up, catalogue in hand.

"She's only bringing a few proposals," Maa said one morning over chai. "Just in case."

Just in case.

As if marriage were a backup plan.

As if Meera's life needed urgent fixing.

As if time was slipping through invisible fingers.

A week later, Meera stood at the station.

Her bag held clothes, books, and something heavier: her right to choose.

Delhi blurred behind her.

Familiar lanes, tea stalls, bus stops—all blurred into motion.

She wasn't just leaving a city.

She was shedding skin, leaving behind the version of herself who had waited.

Waited to be asked. Waited to be chosen. Waited to be told it was okay.

What lay ahead in Bangalore wasn't just a job.

It wasn't just Aman.

It was a possibility.

It was freedom.

It was hers.

Her decision.

Her defiance.

Her declaration.

She was no longer hoping to be someone's reason.

She had become her own.

It was her choice, her freedom to choose.

The first night in Bangalore was anything but quiet.

The breeze outside moved like someone walking barefoot—soft, unhurried, thick with the scent of rain that had touched somewhere nearby. The air inside the room was still, almost thoughtful, the ceiling fan clicking softly, stretching the moment into something sacred.

Meera and Pooja lay on their beds, one window open to the breath of the night, voices slipping easily between them like a well-worn scarf passed across years.

They had wandered through school and college corridors together, growing from girls whispering secrets in history class to women now standing at thresholds. They had shared Maggi, crushes, and heartbreaks. They knew each other's mothers' moods and brothers' names. They belonged to each other's lives, not loudly, not daily, but fully.

And now, in Bangalore, it felt like nothing had changed.

Pooja's voice broke the lull. "You're really here," she said, half in disbelief. "Delhi finally let you go."

Meera hugged a pillow, the fabric warm beneath her fingers. "It still feels strange," she said, her eyes fixed on the ceiling, as if the blades could stir up some courage.

Pooja turned, smiling. "You finally did it. After all those long letters, those weekend calls full of 'what ifs', you finally jumped."

Meera smiled, but it came with the echo of something tender. "Baba made it easier," she said.

Just like that, her mind drifted back to that soft Delhi evening and the courtyard lit in the amber hush before nightfall.

Baba had been standing beneath the peepal tree, not some grand monument, just the familiar one in their courtyard, the one that had always been there like an elder who didn't speak unless needed.

It had watched her grow. It had heard her muttered prayers, her arguments with herself, and the poems she never read aloud.

That evening, Baba didn't say much. He didn't raise his voice or lower it. He just looked at her, long enough for her to know that he saw her fully—not the daughter he imagined, but the woman she was trying to become.

And in that silence, something shifted.

Not control. Not permission.

But something quieter.

A letting go that didn't feel like abandonment.

A trust that didn't need proof.

Like he had taken his hands off the kite, not because he didn't care where it flew, but because he finally believed it knew how to fly.

Meera blinked back into the room, the fan still spinning, the city outside still alive in its gentle chaos.

And for the first time in weeks, maybe months, she didn't feel like she was running.

She felt like she had arrived.

For the first time, she was on her own.

But even here, in the unfamiliar warmth of a Bangalore night, she could feel it —

Baba's faith had travelled with her.

Not like luggage, not like duty.

But like breath.

Unseen, but always arriving.

That evening, holding the sun like it was afraid to let go, she had stood at the gate, bags by her feet, nerves coiled like thread around her spine.

Baba looked at her.

Then past her.

Then toward the old peepal tree.

His voice came steady, like the sound of rain on tin.

"Meera," he had said, holding out a package wrapped in paper like patience.

Inside was a leather-bound notebook, smooth at the edges, the kind that doesn't just hold words but waits for them.

"A new journal," he said, "for a new beginning."

She remembered how his eyes didn't flinch as he continued, "You've been given freedom, my girl. But freedom comes with responsibility. Don't take either lightly. Write your journey in this—your lessons, your mistakes, your victories. Let it remind you that you hold the pen. That you're the writer of your story."

She hugged him hard.

Baba had never been one for long goodbyes, but this time, his arms stayed around her a moment longer, as if memory needed an extra second to fasten itself in place.

Maa stood close. She didn't speak at first, just cupped Meera's face, fingers warm like prayer, eyes glassy like the sky before it weeps. "Take care of yourself," she said, her voice barely louder than a breath.

"I will, Maa," Meera whispered, hoping she sounded surer than she felt.

Raju, always chaos and crumbs, was suddenly quiet. He pressed himself to her waist, his arms a soft grip. "I'll miss you, Didi."

She laughed, trying to keep it light.

She ruffled his hair. "And you, don't trouble Maa too much, okay?"

Raju gave her a wobbly salute, his mouth caught between a smile and a sniffle.

She looked at them one last time —

Baba, still as stone.

Maa, hands folded in the small ache of parting.

Raju, shifting like his feet were unsure of the ground.

And then, her eyes found the peepal tree.

She lifted a hand.

Not just to them.

But to it.

That tree had held her secrets.

It had heard her scribbled dreams, her unsent letters, her silent arguments with the world.

It had watched her grow, leaf by leaf.

And now it stood, still and knowing, as she stepped toward everything she didn't yet know how to name.

And then, she left.

The soft glow of the PG room pulled her back to the present, its yellow hush folding over them like the last light of evening settling on still water.

Pooja's voice drifted through the stillness, careful not to startle it. "What are you thinking about?"

Meera turned slightly, the mattress creaking under her. "I thought Aman would be at the station today," she said, each word like a thread unspooling.

"I don't know… I just assumed."

She had pictured it—his face breaking through the blur of strangers, that familiar smirk, the way it always steadied her, bringing her chaos to rest.

He hadn't come.

The space where he should've stood remained untouched, like a missed step on a staircase.

Pooja rolled onto her side, a small grin tugging at her mouth. "That's because he doesn't know you're in Bangalore."

Meera blinked. "Wait—what?"

Pooja's grin grew, blooming in the dimness like mischief at dusk.

"He still thinks you're in Delhi, overthinking things, stuck in the same loop, rehearsing every 'what if'. Which makes it perfect—we're surprising him on Sunday. Just imagine his face."

Sunday.

The word landed like a stone in water, rippling outward, unsettling everything. Now that she was here, not in another city but just a few streets away, the waiting felt different.

Not lighter.

Heavier, almost.

Urgent.

She exhaled slowly, trying to iron the edges of her nerves.

But the tension stayed, folded neatly beneath her ribs like a secret.

Pooja nudged her shoulder. "Don't be so impatient. It's going to be fun. The surprise. The drama. Classic."

Meera smiled, faint and hesitant. "Maybe," she murmured.

But something in her stayed quiet.

Maybe it would be fun.

Maybe it would be cinematic, a scene to remember.

Or maybe, it would be something else entirely.

When Meera woke, the city was already breathing.

Not loudly, just enough.

A low murmur of life: distant traffic, the rustle of a sheet against her ankle, the low symphony of autos arguing with the morning.

She blinked.

This wasn't home.

It was Saturday, her first full day in Bangalore, her first day of everything.

Across the room, in the tiny kitchenette that was barely a corner, Pooja moved with a rhythm Meera had always known, like a song that never needed remembering.

There were two cups of chai in her hands, steam rising like tiny offerings to the sun.

"Good morning, sleepyhead," Pooja grinned, her voice as warm as the cup she passed. In the other hand, she held a paper packet, already soft from the journey.

"Guess what? Coconut cookies. Your obsession. Drink your tea before the day steals the heat."

Meera sat up slowly, sleep still sitting heavy in her bones.

The cup came into her palms like a familiar truth.

Steam curled upward, fragrant with cardamom and ginger, and for a moment, it felt like Delhi had folded itself into this morning.

She smiled, not a big one but a private curl of the lips, the kind that happens when memory holds hands with comfort.

"Well, at least some things don't change," she said, taking a sip. "Chai still tastes like home."

She looked at Pooja with mock suspicion.

"And you, you're basically Maa. Just without the 6 a.m. 'Rise and shine, *beta*' soundtrack."

Pooja rolled her eyes, still grinning. "Please. I've got better dreams than being your alarm clock."

By the time sunlight had brightened the corners of the room, Pooja was already dressed, in energy and in purpose.

With her bag slung over her shoulder, she lingered at the door with the air of someone who'd done this part a hundred times.

"Enjoy your lazy day," she said with a smirk. Then, gesturing toward the stove, she added, "*Poha's* in the pan. Eat something. For lunch—Maggi. Top shelf. I'm not coming home to a dramatic faint."

Meera groaned, grabbed a pillow, and lobbed it in slow rebellion.

"Yes, Mother," she muttered into the cup.

Pooja ducked effortlessly. "That's more like it," she said, tossing it back, before stepping into the noise and pulse of the city.

And just like that, Meera was alone.

But not quite.

The chai was still warm, the cookie, half-eaten.

And the day, still unwritten.

Without Pooja's voice filling the space, the silence returned like a visitor too familiar to startle, too heavy to ignore.

It settled over the room in layers, not loud, not sharp, just there.

Like steam on glass. Like absence wearing the clothes of peace.

Meera reached for the book on the bedside table, not to read it but to hold something with weight. But the words wouldn't stay. They blurred, floated, and slipped like fish through a net.

Her mind wandered to Aman, then to Delhi. Then, to the echo of her father's voice from the night before, low and slow, like water poured carefully into a glass.

"Take care of yourself, Meera," Baba had said. "Don't overthink. Don't hold back. Just keep moving forward. And don't worry about us. We're always right here."

She had closed her eyes then, just as she did now, letting his words fall into her chest, soft as wool on winter skin.

Warmth that asked for nothing in return.

After a while, she set the book aside and stood up.

There it was again, that slow, creeping restlessness that tiptoed in when everything else grew quiet.

She knew it well.

So, she moved.

She made the bed, not perfectly but just enough. She folded a few clothes, touched the edges of books, and straightened their spines like they mattered.

It wasn't about order.

It was about rhythm and movement. It was about making the stillness earn its place.

By noon, hunger arrived, not loudly, but with insistence. She wandered to the kitchenette, letting her eyes trace the supplies Pooja had left, each item placed with the care of someone who knew the shape of their friend's chaos.

Cooking had always felt like a second language Meera never learned. Chopping vegetables, measuring spices—it all seemed like too many verbs for one act.

So, she chose Maggi—dependable, undemanding, the comfort food of a generation raised between deadlines and dreams.

As the noodles curled in the boiling water, a memory rose, unasked but not unwelcome.

Maa's voice, from another kitchen, another life: "The way to a man's heart is through his stomach." The line was wrapped in a sigh, always aimed with love but laced with judgement.

Meera, indifferent to spice ratios and knife skills, would shrug.

And then, always, Baba's voice, a balm to her mother's fire: "Cooking isn't rocket science. She'll learn when she needs to. Let her be."

That scene had played on loop through the years, as familiar as the ticking of the old wall clock in their courtyard.

Sometimes Meera would wonder aloud that maybe she'd end up with someone who cooked, marinated joy, and plated affection.

She'd laugh and taste, say things like "Too much salt" or "Perfect, love," while never lifting a ladle.

Maa would roll her eyes, muttering, "As if such men grow on trees."

With the bowl of Maggi in her hands, steam rising like a small offering, Meera walked to the window and sat down.

The city stretched below her in motion: men with purpose in their steps, vendors with worn voices hawking fruit and fate.

None of them knew her name.

Not yet.

She took a bite.

It wasn't homesickness, not quite.

But there was something in the stillness of that room, in the solitary slurp of noodles, and in the hum of Bangalore carrying on without her that made her feel like she'd stepped into a space not yet hers.

A threshold. A page mid-turn.

And in that moment, it was enough to just be here.

Breathing. Beginning.

It was 5:30 pm when the door opened, not loudly, just enough to shift the air in the room.

The sound pulled her back from her thoughts.

Pooja stepped in, kicking off her sandals at the door, the day still clinging to her skin like heat after a long walk home.

Her bag hit the floor with a soft thud.

"How was your day?" she asked, her voice loose around the edges, already unwinding.

Meera stretched her arms above her head. "Uneventful," she said. "But I think I needed uneventful."

Pooja dropped onto the bed beside her, body folding like it knew this place, this moment, was safe.

She grinned. "Enjoy the quiet. Tomorrow, we surprise Aman."

Just the sound of his name—that familiar weight—and Meera's stomach fluttered strangely.

Tomorrow.

Pooja nudged her knee. "Nervous?"

"A little," Meera said, her voice small.

"Good," Pooja said, her smile quieter now. "It means he still matters."

Dusk came slowly, soft as a shawl slipping from shoulders. The tiffin arrived in steel containers—warm *dal, aloo gobi, chapatis* wrapped in thin cloth to keep them soft.

Pooja opened the lids like she was lifting the top off something sacred.

"A proper North Indian tiffin in Bangalore!" she said, mock reverent. "Miracles do exist. Let's not waste it."

They sat on the floor, cross-legged, bending toward the food and each other.

Outside, the city moved—horns, voices, the endless exhale of motion—but inside, there was stillness.

Or maybe something better: the silence that knows it's not alone.

The food tasted like home, not the home of address and walls, but the one made of spices, of hand-rolled chapatis, of warmth that lived in flavour.

The kind of home that enters your mouth and stays in your chest.

Pooja talked, the way people do when they're finally offstage. She narrated stories of colleagues, of office drama, of people with too many opinions and too few answers. Her voice moved like wind, soft, always shifting, filling corners Meera hadn't realized were empty.

Later, in bed, with the light off and the ceiling above her just another sky, Meera lay still.

Tomorrow.

She would see him.

Would it feel like stepping back into something once hers, like a coat worn in another winter, or would it feel foreign, like trying on someone else's life?

Would he still be the boy she remembered?

Or had time changed them both in quiet, invisible ways?

She didn't have the answers.

But lying there, listening to the hum of the fan and Pooja's even breath beside her, she knew one thing.

She was ready to find out.

Sunday arrived like a held breath, quiet, golden, trembling at the edges. The city outside hadn't yet found its voice, only a hush broken by the occasional rattle of a bicycle bell, the low bark of a street dog, the light yawn of a world waking too slowly.

Inside, Meera and Pooja stirred in the softened stillness, wrapped not in duvets but in the thrum of what the day held. This wasn't just another Sunday folded into the calendar; this one had a pulse. A secret folded inside it. Today, they would surprise Aman.

Since that conversation in Delhi—Pooja's voice low across a tinny phone line, saying he seemed different now, more distant—the thought of this day had looped quietly in Meera's head, like music that plays long after it's stopped. And now, it was here. Tactile. Breathing.

She dressed slowly, as if dressing was part ritual, part armour. She wore a soft pink *chikan* kurta, its threads delicate as breath, matched with cotton pants. No sparkle, no noise. Just fabric that understood her silence. In the mirror, she caught sight of herself—eyes not entirely sure but awake in some new way. Nervous. Expectant. Almost unfamiliar. She wondered if Aman would see that. Would he know what it took to show up like this?

Across the room, Pooja was already in motion, pacing like a wound-up toy, toast in one hand, a grin spread wide across her face. There was mischief in her steps, joy tucked behind every gesture. She looked like a child about to pull off a magic trick she'd been rehearsing for weeks.

"Are you ready?" she asked, already knowing the answer.

Meera didn't speak. She only nodded slowly and deliberately. Because "ready" wasn't a word; it was a weight. And today, it sat differently on her shoulders.

"Today's going to be epic," Pooja said between bites, butter glistening on her toast like sunlight on glass. "The look on his face when he sees you will be priceless. He might forget to sulk for once."

Meera rolled her eyes, but her lips betrayed her, lifting just slightly, like the sun catching the edge of a closed curtain. Stunned? Maybe. Happy? That was harder to wish for. The last time she had imagined seeing Aman was at the train station. That moment was now blurred, like a photo developed incorrectly, the colours not quite real.

But today wouldn't vanish, not like that.

She would hold today.

They stepped out and flagged an auto rickshaw, its engine coughing like an old man woken too early. The city yawned around them, the streets half dreaming, half waking. It was 10 a.m., and the roads had not yet remembered to hurry. Scooters hummed by, unbothered. A flower vendor unpacked marigolds like memories, and dogs stretched out like unanswered questions in the sun. The air was steeped in morning—hot *idlis* steaming from roadside stalls, coffee thick as truth, the clatter of a city trying to become itself again.

Twenty minutes passed in that suspended rhythm.

Finally, they stood outside Aman's apartment, a weathered 2BHK tucked at the end of a sleepy lane, given to him by his uncle, not as a gift wrapped in ribbon, but as something practical, expected. A place to stay. The building looked like it had exhaled and forgotten to breathe back in. The walls were faded, the paint peeling in the corners like old regrets. The staircase groaned beneath its own memory.

Her eyes found it—*Aman Verma*, etched in plain black on a nameplate screwed slightly askew, the letters not proud, just there. Her gaze drifted up, finally, to the closed door—simple, wooden, waiting.

Not an invitation. Not yet.

Just a door.

Pooja, already familiar with this place from past visits, stepped forward without pause and rang the bell.

Silence answered first.

Then came the wait, stretched and slow, the kind that wraps around your ribs and tightens.

Still nothing.

Meera stood there, the air thick around her.

A pause can be a sentence. And this one said too much.

Then, finally, the door opened.

Aman stood there, not startled, not calm either, just still, as if time had opened the door instead of him. He didn't speak. His eyes landed on her, startled but not surprised. Or maybe surprised in the way a person is when they remember something they meant to forget.

Pooja, out of sight, let the moment belong to the two of them.

Meera didn't move. She hadn't rehearsed this part—what to say, where to look, how to stand. There had never been hugs between them, no blueprint for affection. And yet, something inside her reached forward, not for touch, but for recognition.

That would've been enough.

But Aman didn't offer either.

His expression held, flat, unreadable, except for the briefest flicker in his eyes. A shift. Like a door creaking open, only to shut again just as fast. She couldn't tell what passed through him. Was it surprise? Was it discomfort? Was it memory? Or was it just habit?

He looked at her, then at Pooja, connecting the dots.

Still no words.

Pooja broke the hush. "Surprise! What, you thought you could hide forever?"

She stepped forward, gesturing toward Meera. "Look who I brought—your silent rescue crew. But don't panic. You know Meera. She won't drag you out of your cave. She'll just sit at the mouth and wait till you decide to step out."

Aman blinked once. A breath escaped him, small and tired at the edges. Then the barest smile, more fatigue than joy, played on his mouth.

"It's good to see you," he said. Quietly. Almost to himself.

Before the silence could return, Pooja clapped her hands. "So, what's the plan? Are we standing here till lunchtime, or are you going to let us in?"

Aman stepped aside.

"Come in," he said.

Meera stepped in slowly, the air folding around her like a held breath.

Light filtered through half-drawn curtains, a tired kind of gold, settling on the floor like it had nowhere else to go.

The room was clean, but not the kind of clean that invites you in.

Clean like no one had stayed long enough to leave behind a mess.

A couch slumped against the wall. Two mismatched chairs were placed beside it. There was a coffee table in the centre, with an old newspaper folded sharply, as if it was still waiting to be read.

The walls were empty, not white but silent, the kind of silent that forgets you were ever there.

Even the kitchen gleamed, not from love but from habit. Steel pots were placed in a line, the counters so still they seemed afraid to be used.

Aman gestured toward the chairs by the window. "Make yourselves comfortable," he said, turning toward the kitchen.

He reached for a pan, the gesture automatic. But Pooja was there, her hand light on his wrist.

"Ah!" she said, smiling, taking over. "I know you think you're the chef here, but today, it's me."

Aman let go easily, that small ghost of a smile rising to the surface.

"I'm not used to having guests," he said. "At least, let me pretend to know what I'm doing."

Pooja lit the stove like it was a familiar ritual. "Well, get used to it. We're going to be around so much you won't remember whose place this is."

She winked at Meera. "Right?"

Rolling up her sleeves, she tossed Aman a look over her shoulder.

"You can supervise, if that helps your ego."

Then she said to Meera, "Can you believe it? Aman Verma, a guest in his own kitchen!"

Meera smiled, soft at the edges. But her eyes were elsewhere—on the stillness, the bare corners.

It wasn't just the walls that were empty.

It was the air, too.

As if no one had breathed fully here in a long time.

Her voice came without warning. "So…for how long have you been living here?"

Aman looked up and shrugged, just a little. "A few months, I think."

She nodded. Her gaze floated back to the pale wall behind him.

"It still feels…" She paused. "Empty. Maybe some colour would make it feel more alive."

As soon as she said it, she wished she hadn't. The words felt too direct, like fingers brushing something too raw.

She looked away, her breath catching in her throat.

Aman ran a hand through his hair. "Colour won't do it," he said, almost to himself. "A painting might brighten a wall, but it won't make it a home."

Pooja laughed softly, pouring the tea now, her eyes warm with mischief.

"Then maybe it's not colour you need," she said. "Maybe it's company."

She placed the cups gently on the table. "Some people bring the colour with them."

Meera looked at Aman. Really looked.

And for a moment, something small and warm stirred inside her, like a match struck in a dark room.

Maybe Pooja was right.

It was never the paintings or the flowers.

A home was made of people who stayed long enough to leave warmth behind.

Who filled a room not with things, but with presence.

She wondered if Aman knew, if somewhere beneath all that stillness he remembered what it felt like to let someone in.

To let a space hold more than silence.

Maybe, just maybe, there was still a light in him that hadn't gone out.

A place inside him that still had room.

For return.

For beginning again.

For her.

The chai was still warm.

Not cold, just paused, like a breath held too long.

Its sweetness still hung in the room, but the stillness had settled, thick and unmoving.

A hush not born of emptiness, but of everything left unsaid.

Meera's eyes drifted to the two cups on the table, chipped at the edges, the colour dulled with time.

She wondered if, one day, there would be cups that bloomed in her hands, their colours loud and unapologetic.

Curtains that fluttered, not just to keep the light out but to let something in.

Books, stacked not in corners but in hearts.

Music, not to fill a void but to celebrate its ending.

Laughter that lingered long after the moment had passed.

Maybe one day, she would bring warmth, not just into the room but into him.

Aman didn't move.

Stillness was his first language.

Next came silence.

Pooja, brave and bright, kept the air alive, tossing questions like flowers, letting her voice move freely across the room.

Meera sat between them—between what was and what could be.

A girl in the middle of a room, her body present, but her mind somewhere between a past that never unfolded and a future still writing itself.

Hope curled in her chest like smoke from a match she didn't mean to light.

Then, a clap, sharp and familiar, cracked the quiet.

"Meera, you've got that interview tomorrow!" Pooja's voice was sunshine cracking through shutters.

"But before that, you need to fall in love with this city."

She was grinning now, wide and sure.

"You're not a visitor anymore. You're moving here. Soak it in. Let it lift you. Let it carry you when you walk into that room tomorrow."

Aman turned slightly, his eyes lifting toward Meera, then to Pooja. "How many more surprises are you hiding?" he asked.

His voice was calm, but something lived in it—something fragile, almost leaning forward.

Like a door left slightly ajar.

Curiosity, maybe.

Or hope trying on its shape.

Pooja grinned, her mischief blooming like jasmine in the heat. "Oh, there are plenty of secrets, but I'm saving some. Meera gets to break them to you eventually."

Meera felt the flick of panic, sharp, like a match struck too close to skin.

What if Pooja said something—something real, something too much?

But her friend only winked, sealing her silence with a smile.

Relief pooled in her chest. And beside it, disappointment, soft as dusk.

Pooja clapped her hands. "Enough of this domestic tea party. Let's step out. Cubbon Road's calling! Meera, you'll love it."

And she did.

The moment her foot touched the pavement, something unlocked within her.

The city, for once, didn't press in; it opened.

The air felt looser here, like it had learned not to rush.

Trees lined the road like old friends standing at attention.

Colonial buildings whispered the stories of past lives, and in between them, the rhythm of Bangalore—slow, steady, sure—beat like a second heart.

They walked unhurriedly. Pooja was no longer just a friend but a guide with widely sweeping arms and a loud voice.

"That's the State Library! And that little shack? It has the best filter coffee in Bangalore—fight me!"

Aman walked beside them, his words folded inside his pockets.

He answered when asked, but his eyes didn't settle; they searched past the crowd, past the sky, like memory had called, and he couldn't help but answer.

Meera watched him, the way a leaf watches the wind.

"You always loved discovering new places," she said softly.

Aman turned, his smile crooked, worn like an old photograph.

"Maybe I just ran out of places to explore."

Before silence could bloom again, Pooja broke it, as she always did, like the sun breaking through the wrong side of the window.

"Lunch time! *Idli-sambar*! No arguments."

The café was tucked behind a rusted signboard, but inside, the smell of home swam in the air—hot sambar, toasted red masala, steamed comfort.

Pooja placed a hand dramatically on her heart. "This," she declared, "is what true happiness tastes like."

Meera laughed, and this time, it wasn't the polite kind.

It spilled from her, golden and whole, the kind of laugh that leaves you fuller than food.

She hadn't known she was hungry for this—not just the idli, not just the heat, but this ease.

This gentle sense of home that asked for nothing but her presence.

Even Aman seemed slightly relaxed now, the weight on his shoulders no longer anchored.

He tapped the table with two fingers, no rhythm, just presence.

Meera noticed the change.

And that glimpse of movement mattered.

They stayed, letting the conversation meander like a river that wasn't in a hurry.

Old memories, bad jokes, broken punchlines—anything but the silences they'd all been carrying, like suitcases too heavy to unpack.

Later, as Pooja floated the idea of Ulsoor Lake or Commercial Street, Aman glanced at his watch.

"Let's not wear Meera out," he said lightly. "She's got her interview tomorrow. She needs to be well rested."

Meera's heart pulled.

She wanted, with a kind of ache that lived in her ribs, for him to say more.

To say: "Because once you clear it, you'll stay… because I want you here. With me."

But he didn't.

And maybe that was enough for now.

Maybe some hopes are meant to be spoken softly, like a bird that only sings when no one's listening.

She almost whispered, "I wouldn't feel tired in your company. Not ever."

But the words remained sealed behind her lips, warm, afraid, still learning how to be brave.

"Oh, come on, Aman," Pooja laughed, nudging him with her elbow. "It's not like she's appearing for the UPSC or something."

It should've been harmless, light. But the air around them shifted, sharp, sudden.

Pooja bit her lip too late. The joke had already cut, already reached the part of him it shouldn't have touched.

Aman didn't flinch. He didn't need to. His silence folded inward, like a door slowly closing. His eyes moved, just a little, away from her, away from them, toward something he thought was private.

But Meera saw it—that flicker, like a match lit in a cave, burning only long enough to remind you of the dark.

She said nothing. She didn't have to. There are some wounds language cannot hold, only witness.

Pooja and Meera climbed into an auto. The city moved past them in soft, unfinished shapes. Meera looked back once instinctively.

Aman stood where they'd left him, still as a question unanswered. He looked smaller than he did when they were younger, not in body but in spirit.

Like someone who had once belonged to something and no longer did. Someone untethered, like a kite flying too long without wind.

The auto hummed, filling the silence between the two girls that didn't need words to feel heavy.

Even Pooja, so full of colour, was silent, her brightness dimmed under the weight of her own slip.

But Meera's mind was loud. She thought of Aman—the way he used to walk with purpose, like he had somewhere to be, someone to become.

Now, he moved through the world like it owed him nothing. And maybe he believed that now.

The waiting room was too cold, the kind of cold that didn't belong here, a chill bred by machines, not the monsoon. Air conditioning was still rare then, more myth than norm, and it made Meera feel alert in a way that wasn't entirely welcome.

Outside, Bangalore moved—buses groaned, bells rang, the world kept going. But in here, everything slowed as if breath had been held.

She sat on the stiff couch near the reception, her folder resting on her lap like something sacred or fragile. Her fingers tapped along its edge, restless, unable to stay still.

The interview was over, that strange little theatre of performance and guessing.

Now came the real part: waiting.

She replayed it all, the way we do, turning each word over like a stone, wondering what might have lived beneath it.

"Tell me about yourself."

She had smiled, too politely, maybe. A schoolgirl smile, the kind you wear when you're trying to be taken seriously.

"I grew up in Delhi, in a small home that smelled of chai and evening news. My father is a head clerk, a man of quiet discipline and quiet dreams. My mother is a homemaker who managed everything with very little, teaching me what care and resilience really mean.

"I studied literature at Delhi University. That's where I began noticing things more closely—how a silence could speak, how a sentence could hold a person. I don't have a portfolio, but I write in a journal, mostly. Not for anyone else, just to understand the world and my place in it."

They nodded. Or maybe they didn't. Faces are hard to read when you're trying too hard.

"What made you apply for this role?"

She felt clearer here. Her voice was steadier.

"I've always believed everyone has a story. That's what drew me to Media House, the idea that stories can move people, shift something inside them. I want to be part of that process, not just writing but building something meaningful, something that lasts.

"I think good stories do that—they stay. And I want to learn how to tell them well with honesty and care."

There was another pause. Someone looked through her resume, as if it held secrets she didn't know were in it.

"How do you think you'll add value here?"

She'd taken a breath, held it like a prayer.

"I listen. I notice the small things. And I think that helps me find the heart of a story. I may not come with experience, but I come with curiosity, discipline, and a need to understand people—what matters to them, what moves them. I'm not here just to take up a role; I'm here to tell stories that stay, stories that mean something."

And then, it ended. Softly. No applause. Just breathe again.

The receptionist typed without looking up. Someone in a navy suit walked past twice, as if retracing their own nerves. Meera glanced at the wall clock. Five minutes. Ten. Time bends in places like this.

She leaned back, folder clutched tight, telling herself not to hope too much, not to care too much.

But it's hard to do so. Hope doesn't listen.

Then the door opened.

A woman stepped out, green silk catching the overhead light. She didn't need to speak; the space around her shifted with her presence. Her ID card swung once, twice: Kavita Singh, HR Head.

Meera sat up straight, eyes flicking to her face, looking for a sign, any shape of the future.

Kavita's smile was calm and practised.

"Congratulations, Meera," she said. "You've been selected."

Meera's breath caught, not loudly, just enough to be felt like the first drop of rain on a dry road.

"When can you join?" Kavita asked.

"Right away," Meera answered. The words flew out before her doubts could catch them.

Kavita's smile widened slightly. "Good. You start today. Collect your appointment letter from the reception. Report to your department."

Neha was behind the desk—crisp navy blouse, hair pulled back, a calm efficiency in her fingers. She looked up and smiled the way people do when they've already heard the news.

"Congratulations," she said, handing over an envelope like it was a doorway. "It looks like we'll be seeing you around."

Meera took it with careful, measured movements, still floating somewhere between disbelief and a beginning. "I guess so," she murmured.

"Well, well, look at you. First day at work already?"

That voice. Familiar, bright.

She turned.

Pooja stood there, arms folded, grin wide, like an older sister watching a younger one finally step into the light.

Meera laughed, the sound small, surprised. "It looks like we're going to be colleagues."

"More than that," Pooja said, looping her arm through Meera's. "Your desk is right next to mine."

"Seriously?" Meera blinked, a little stunned by how suddenly something heavy in her had lifted.

"Seriously," Pooja smiled, already pulling her forward. "Come on. Let me show you the kingdom you're about to rule."

Meera followed, the folder still in her hand, the offer letter still warm from the print. Her heart struggled to catch up with her steps.

Just three days ago, this city had felt like too much—too wide, too strange, too fast. But now, with Pooja beside her and a job she hadn't dared to dream of, something changed. Softened.

She hadn't meant to stay. That was the promise she had made to herself. She was here to breathe, to pause, to visit Aman, and even that had felt like asking for too much.

She had no degree or internship. Just a worn-out journal and a quiet wish. She told herself she was just passing through.

But maybe there had always been a different story trying to be written.

And now, here she was, walking down corridors lined with soft white light. The paper in her hand read something she still couldn't believe:

You've been chosen.

Not because she fit perfectly, but because she dared to ask.

The city, once vast and distant, seemed to breathe with her, quiet, patient, waiting, as if to say: This is where you start.

And then, a voice. Low. Casual. "New hire?"

She turned. A man stood a few feet away, sleeves rolled up, a coffee mug steaming in his hand. He looked like someone who didn't need to try to be noticed and didn't care if he was.

Pooja was quick to respond. "Yes. Meet Meera."

He glanced at her. Just one second, one nod. "Welcome to the team. I'm Aman Rana. Team Lead."

Meera's breath caught, not in a romantic way, but in the way when you stumble across a name you once kept close. Aman. But no, not him. This was someone else. Another life, another story.

He turned back to his desk, already gone from the moment.

Pooja nudged her, that familiar sparkle in her eyes. "What a good-looking boss we've got! But just because his name is Aman, don't think he's yours."

Meera smiled softly, shaking her head. "You can have him all to yourself. I'm not here to compete."

"Oh, how generous!" Pooja said, mock-swooning, hand over her heart. "We'd make quite the pair, though, right? A real power couple."

And just like that, the moment folded into something small and golden—two friends, laughter tucked between new beginnings. The hallway, once unfamiliar, now hummed with the low, steady pulse of belonging.

As Meera settled at her desk, the chair still unfamiliar beneath her, a quiet ache crept in, the kind that comes when you leave something behind that you love. She already missed home: Maa's bangles clinking in the kitchen, Baba's slow footsteps in the hallway, the smell of cardamom rising with the morning tea. Delhi wasn't across the world, but today, it felt that way.

And yet, there was something about being here, in this new city, in this new skin, that held her still. Maybe it was the job. Maybe it was the rhythm of a beginning. Maybe it was simply the chance to stay.

She didn't know what would come next. But she was here now. And as the hum of the office carried on around her, something still and certain inside whispered:

Stay a little longer. You belong.

The months slipped past faster than Meera expected. Bangalore wasn't a pause anymore. It was not home, not quite, but it was something she could hold onto.

She found her rhythm here—the auto drivers who didn't take advantage, the quiet streets when the city screamed rush hour, the little shop heavy with the smell of rain and old books piled to the ceiling.

Work kept her steady, but it was the small things, the moments between, that told her time was moving. Coffee runs with Pooja after late shifts. Sundays spent sprawled on the floor with Pooja and Aman, laughing at sitcoms even when the antenna cracked. Flea market walks where she bargained for earrings she'd never wear. The laughter, the teasing, and the routines settled like a soft song playing just beneath the noise.

Every few days, she'd slip into the corner STD booth near her place. She knew Baba would be home, waiting.

She pictured him there—leaning back in his old chair, the fan above humming low, a folded newspaper by his side.

Sometimes Maa would pick up, her voice threaded with love and worry.

"Are you eating well, beta?"

"Yes, Maa."

"You sound tired."

"I'm fine. Just a long day."

But mostly, it was Baba she spoke to. He listened more than he talked. Shared small advice gently. Reminded her she was stronger than she knew. That even in a city so far from home, she was never truly alone.

Those calls were her tether, her pause in the rush, her anchor.

Now, sitting across from Pooja in the café, Meera stirred sugar into the steel cup, her movements slow and deliberate. The air between them held something unspoken, waiting to unfold.

Pooja exhaled, tracing the mug's edge with her finger.

"Meera, I have to say something."

Meera looked up with a half smile, light in her eyes.

"That sounds serious."

Pooja paused. A small, uncertain smile.

"Simran didi's expecting. Maa wants me to stay with her for a few months, at least."

The words settled in the silence between them.

"You're moving in with her? When?"

"In a week, maybe less." Pooja's voice softened. "I've been thinking… about you. I don't want you to be alone."

Something clenched inside Meera's chest. Alone, a word she'd never lived with. Not even for a night. The silence of solitude was foreign to her.

She tried to shrug it off. "I guess I could try living alone."

Pooja raised an eyebrow. A teasing laugh.

Meera narrowed her eyes. "Don't look at me like that."

Pooja smiled mischievously. "Do you remember that horror movie? How you made me keep the lights on for three nights?"

Meera groaned, stirring in more sugar, sweetening the coffee more than she meant to. A small rebellion against the knot tightening in her chest.

She wanted to believe she could do it.

"Maybe it'll be hard, at first," she said, "but I'll get used to it."

Pooja leaned in, her voice soft but steady.

"What if something happens? Or you just feel… off? I know you, Meera. You hide when you're scared. This city is still new to you. I don't want to leave you like that."

Meera's silence said everything.

After a long pause, Pooja spoke again, her voice quieter, careful. "There might be another way."

Meera looked up, wary. "What way?"

Pooja hesitated, then said carefully, "Aman."

Meera blinked, the name brushing her like wind through a crack in the window.

"Aman?"

Pooja nodded slowly, like the name itself carried weight. "He has a two-bedroom flat. And it's not like he's a stranger. He's… solid, Meera. You know that. If there's anyone you'd feel safe around, it's him."

Meera leaned back. Her body stayed still, but something inside scattered.

Aman. The name unsettled the air.

He was steady in a way the city wasn't. He was the kind of man who poured water before being asked. Who listened without filling the silence. Who stood near but never too near, like he knew the shape of space she needed.

But to live with him?

"I don't know…" she started. Her voice came out smaller than she meant.

Pooja leaned in, like she could hold Meera's doubt in her palms. "Just think about it logically. You need a place. He has one. If it were anyone else, I wouldn't even bring it up. But this is Aman. You know he'd never cross a line."

Meera stared down, the coffee in her tumbler turning cold. She trusted him. That wasn't the problem.

It was herself.

The way her chest folded in when he looked at her—really looked. The quiet pauses between his words, where her breath forgot what to do.

Could she live beside that, night after night, and call it convenience? Then something else came to mind, sharp, sudden. Her parents.

"Pooja… how am I supposed to explain this to Baba and Maa?" Her voice shrank like it knew how deep the question cut. "Baba never says no, but he wouldn't even know how to say yes to this. And Maa… she'd probably faint."

Pooja sighed and put her mug down, like setting down a burden. "You don't have to tell them."

"What?" Meera looked up, eyes wide. "No. I can't just not tell them. I've never lied to Baba."

"I'm not telling you to lie," Pooja said gently. "Just don't tell them everything. Not right now."

Meera's mouth opened, then closed again, a protest swallowed. It wasn't a lie, not really, but it wasn't the truth either.

Would Baba even understand? His world was built on steady ground. Right and wrong. Known and unknown. He'd never lived between lines. To him, a girl moving in with a man, even platonically, was a shadow on a clean wall, a kind of wrong you couldn't explain without making it sound worse.

She could already hear his voice, quiet, disappointed: This isn't how things are done, beta. What will people say? Freedom isn't just about choices; it's about consequences.

But she couldn't blame him. He belonged to a time when rules weren't broken; they were inherited.

Still, Baba had broken one once. He had left his village for the city, disobeying his father to chase a future no one else could see. Meera had heard the story, how her grandfather had said: This isn't our way.

But Baba did it anyway.

Years later, when he sent Meera to college in Delhi, he'd told his father: You may not understand, but I trust her. She just must be responsible.

Now it was her turn, her decision to make, her fire to hold.

Wasn't this her life? Didn't she have to live every part of it—the brave parts, the unsure parts?

Meera pressed her fingertips to her temples. She didn't know how to start that conversation with Baba or explain a freedom wrapped in doubt.

But hadn't he always told her: Write your story. Don't wait for someone else to hold the pen.

Maybe Pooja was right.

Maybe silence, for now, wasn't deceit. Maybe it was shelter.

Pooja saw the flicker cross Meera's face. She reached across the table, her hand warm and steady. "I know it's not easy," she said. "But sometimes you have to do what makes sense for you, not what makes everyone else comfortable."

Meera stared into her coffee, searching its surface like it might crack open and show her a path.

Pooja leaned back, watching her, a smile playing at the edge of her lips. "You trust Aman," she said. "That's not the problem. You just don't trust yourself. That's what's scaring you."

Meera looked up, caught mid-thought, like someone had read her mind.

Pooja smirked. “I thought so.”

Meera turned her gaze to the window, cheeks flushing.

“It’s not like that,” she muttered.

“Sure,” Pooja said, sipping her coffee. “Keep telling yourself that.”

The suitcase hummed softly behind her, its tiny wheels brushing the pavement like a thought she wasn't ready to finish. Meera walked beside Pooja through the hush of the evening, the air thick with things unsaid, like clouds swollen with rain that wouldn't come.

She wasn't overthinking anymore, or so she kept telling herself. This wasn't about principles or proving a point. It was not even about rebellion. It was just… what fit, for now.

Still, her heart hadn't caught up.

The decision hadn't come in a burst. It had unspooled slowly over days, thread by thread—this move, this new space, this closeness she wasn't sure how to name.

With Pooja leaving for her sister's place, Meera had counted her options. There weren't many.

And Aman—he made it look easy.

When Pooja had mentioned the idea, he'd only shrugged.

"If Meera's okay with it, I am, too."

Simple words. Kind words.

But something in her recoiled gently.

Yes, it was her choice. Entirely.

But maybe, just maybe, she didn't want it to be.

She didn't want indifference.

She wanted longing.

She wanted him to want her there, not as a guest, not as someone to make space for, but as someone whose presence mattered.

She ached for that unnamed thing—two lives pressing into one decision, a yes shaped by two mouths.

But Aman wasn't hers, not like that.

Not yet.

And it wasn't fair to ask him for something he never promised.

Still, what could she do about her heart, the silent rebel that leaned without permission?

Outside his apartment, suitcase in hand, her pulse beat a quiet panic against her ribs.

Pooja's voice was soft, like fingers brushing hair from a forehead.

"Are you sure about this? If you're not, if it feels too quick, you can stay at Simran didi's. Just say the word."

Meera's eyes stayed on the door.

"You've seen her flat. It's barely big enough for you. I'd be sleeping next to the fridge."

Pooja gave a small nod.

"I just want you to know you still have choices. You don't have to do this if it's too soon. Even if we both know he's decent, safe. Even if I trust him with my life, if your mind says to wait, listen to it."

Meera said nothing.

Her fingers curled tighter around the suitcase handle, as if the plastic grip could ground her body. As if holding on to something meant she wouldn't fall through this moment.

She took a breath, not deep, not steady, but enough to square her shoulders like armour. Walking through that door wasn't just about changing a pin code; it was stepping into something unnamed, something shaped like Aman but not quite him. Not yet.

"I'll be fine here," she said, mostly to herself. The words barely rose, like steam from a cooling cup. And then, before she could fold the sentence back into silence, the door opened.

Aman stood there in a cotton T-shirt and joggers, that soft, unbothered smile already in place. "It took you both long enough."

Pooja grinned. "Someone's nervous."

Meera shot her a look, sharp and silent.

But Pooja, being Pooja, pushed on. "Or maybe she's waiting for a pot of rice at the doorstep. For good *shagun*, obviously."

Aman laughed, a quiet ripple through the air. Meera groaned. "Pooja, seriously? That's not even a joke."

Still smiling, Aman stepped aside, his arm sweeping toward the hallway like a curtain opening. "Come in. No need to be shy. We both know Pooja. She's incapable of subtlety."

Meera stepped in, and the apartment seemed to envelop her, not suddenly, but gently, like it had been waiting.

It was quiet. Familiar.

The kind of familiarity that didn't comfort her but stirred something low and slow in her chest.

The smell of coffee still hung in the air. His cologne, too, the one she used to catch in passing, now lingered, steady and close.

She had often been here before, on Sundays or unhurried evenings. Just long enough to share a moment or two.

She'd sit in the living room, talk, laugh, or sometimes say nothing at all.

But never with a suitcase in hand.

On the table, a small stack of books awaited, books she loved.

Not arranged by genre or author, but by memory. By care.

He had remembered.

This was his way, quiet and deliberate. A kind of softness that didn't ask to be noticed but stayed anyway.

A way of saying something without saying it.

Maybe he saw her.

Maybe he even wanted her here.

She had always hovered near the edges, never fully in. But now, it felt different. The same walls, the same space, but no longer borrowed.

She wasn't just passing through.

She was part of it.

Maybe not completely.

Maybe not yet.

But for the first time in a long time, it didn't feel only his.

Maybe, with time, it could begin to feel like hers, too.

Maybe, theirs.

Aman walked her to the second room.

"You can take this one," he said, his voice soft as cotton. No performance. No weight.

The room was small.

A bed with a plain cover, a desk waiting for a purpose, a window that opened to a street that didn't yet know her name.

But it felt like enough.

And standing there, she remembered how many times she had been in this apartment and yet never once stepped into this room.

The bedroom had always been a boundary she didn't cross.

That space wasn't hers.

Not then.

But now?

Now, she was here. Not as a guest. Not just visiting.

Aman's voice broke her thoughts.

"It's yours," he said, "for as long as you want."

Meera put her suitcase down, the soft thud louder than it should've been.

"Thank you," she said.

Quiet. Like prayer.

Aman shrugged, almost shy.

"It's no big deal."

But it was.

To her, it was everything.

Before Meera could speak, Pooja sighed, loud and theatrical, like a curtain lifting.

"Oh, come on! Remember that iconic dialogue: 'In friendship, there's no sorry, no thank you.'"

She wiggled her eyebrows, and the words settled like dust in the air between them.

Meera knew the line before Pooja even finished saying it.

Of course she did. They all did.

*Maine Pyar Kiya*, that romantic film from the '90s, lived like a heartbeat for their generation. Salman Khan as Prem, Bhagyashree as Suman. The way their eyes met, the way innocence was caught in soft light. And that one line, this dialogue, flew through their youth like a bridge no one questioned. A rule dressed in romance, friendship draped in cinematic gold. Their generation had been fed that line repeatedly, whispered into late-night phone calls, passed between lovers and friends alike.

Aman laughed. Low, affectionate.

"Trust Pooja to turn everything into a Bollywood reference."

Meera rolled her eyes, but the corners of her mouth betrayed her, something close to a smile forming there, shy as a petal that doesn't know if it belongs to spring.

Before she could even find a reply, Pooja clapped her hands once.

"Alright, the big move is done. I'll leave you two, Prem and Suman, to settle in."

Meera's cheeks warmed, and she quickly looked away, hoping Aman wouldn't notice.

Her head turned too fast. "You're leaving already?"

"Yes," Pooja said, already halfway down the hallway. "You'll be just fine."

After she left, Aman leaned on the doorway, as if leaning on time itself. "You must be hungry," he asked.

Meera blinked.

"A little."

"Same here," he said. "But no rush. Settle in first. When you're ready, we'll go to this café down the lane that does dosas. They're not great, but they're not bad either."

His words made her smile, not because of the dosas but because of the honesty. The simplicity of something offered without trying to impress.

Just...offered.

"Sounds good," she murmured.

He nodded, stepping back like a tide retreating just enough to make room.

And then, it was just her again. Her, the room, and the unfamiliar ache of belonging. She sat on the edge of the bed, the mattress giving way like it knew her presence now.

This was it.

Under his roof. In his air.

A room that waited, even when she didn't know it was waiting.

This wasn't about logistics. It wasn't about shelter. It was about how her body reacted to his, how her pulse whispered secrets before her mind could catch them. It was about the silence between their conversations and how it was filled with something not yet named but deeply known.

Maybe going out for a walk, sitting across from him under the glow of bad lighting, a dosa between them, would be easier than sitting alone in a room that now held both their shadows.

And maybe, just maybe, for tonight, that would be enough.

Moving to Bangalore was never really about the job. That's just what she said when people asked. It made things easier, cleaner. But the truth was softer, more tender. She came here to see what might happen when the walls around her were no longer made of love. At home, everything was ready before it was needed. Her parents gave without asking, sheltered without question. And she was grateful, but also restless. She wanted to know who she was when no one was watching. When no one called her name out of habit or history, in this new city, where the streets didn't know her footsteps. The evenings were hers alone. And maybe that was the point—not to escape home, but to see if she could live outside it. To carry herself, even just a little.

At the office, her words didn't land at first. She turned in articles that came back bleeding with red lines. She stayed late, watched others leave. She rewrote paragraphs under the hum of tube lights, fingertips smudged with ink. She learned how to cut, how to listen. She learned that good writing wasn't always in the idea, but in the return to it.

Sometimes it stung. Sometimes it felt like being slowly erased and drawn again. But still, she stayed.

And slowly, something changed. Her name was mentioned in meetings. A line she wrote stayed on the page. A nod from a senior. Not loud praise, but a quiet kind. The kind you don't notice until it's already inside you.

She started walking a little taller, not because she'd won something, but because she was no longer waiting to be told she could.

Aman's apartment felt like a room paused mid-breath. Nothing unkind, just unfamiliar. She walked softly. Folded things neatly. Placed her toothbrush down softly, like it might wake someone. The silence wasn't cold; it just hadn't learned her yet.

Their conversations were short and functional.

"You're back."

"Long day?"

"Tea?"

Words, like furniture, moved carefully, used just enough.

But something else began. Not in sentences, but in gestures. A light left on. A second towel folded without asking. His voice when he said her name—how it stayed with her a beat longer than the sound itself.

She didn't name it. She didn't want to. Sometimes, naming things makes them disappear.

Evenings were quiet. Aman on the floor, back to the wall, reading. Meera in the chair, book open, unread. The kind of silence that holds rather than empties.

It happened slowly, like dusk folding itself into a room, quiet, steady, unnoticed until it was everywhere. He stopped working late, not with intention, but by degrees. One evening, the files stayed closed; another, the pen rested idle. Deadlines lost their edge, or perhaps he let them soften. Some nights, he simply sat by the window, the city blurring into pools of amber and shadow.

Meera would glance over, catching the unguarded slope of his shoulders, the way his stillness seemed to breathe beside hers. She began to sit differently, too, not as a visitor careful with space, but as someone settling in. Her book lay open but unturned. Her presence was no longer tentative. The silences between them no longer asked to be filled; they simply held.

She didn't ask what he was thinking. But she noticed the way their evenings leaned gently into one another, how comfort replaced caution. Not love, not yet. But something that could become love, if left undisturbed, if allowed to unfold at its own unhurried pace.

She stayed. Not because it was easy, but because, for the first time, she felt herself becoming someone she could trust.

Sundays were different.

Not in loud or obvious ways, but in the way light shifts through a room that's been quiet too long.

Meera and Aman had begun to settle into each other's evenings, but a whole day together still felt like too much space.

The silence wasn't unkind, just unfamiliar, like a hallway you're still learning to walk without echo.

It wasn't that they didn't enjoy being around each other; it was that they hadn't yet figured out how to fill a Sunday.

The hours moved slowly, sometimes awkwardly, as if the day was holding its breath.

But Pooja came, like she always did. Sundays belonged a little to her. She arrived with her usual burst of laughter, bringing out stories, card games, old Ludo boards, and the tape recorder, a birthday gift to Aman from both her and Meera, spinning their weekends into songs. Meera's Kishore Kumar, Pooja's R.D. Burman, Aman's Rafi—the music weaved through the rooms, filling the apartment with a softness that felt like home. Pooja's presence moved through the apartment like wind through sheer curtains, light, familiar, just enough.

With her around, the day softened.

It didn't need effort.

She filled the silences without making them disappear, gave back the room its ease. When she left, she left behind a trace of comfort, a reminder that silence could be kind, too.

Outside, the rain tapped softly and steadily against the glass. Inside, tea simmered slowly, filling the room with warmth. From the stove, the scent of something gentle curled upward. They sat together in the silence. There was no need for words, no plans to make, just the quiet warmth of presence.

Lunch was Aman's small ritual, never fancy, but always careful, like a quiet promise. Some Sundays, when the thought of cooking stretched too far, they'd walk out to a nearby corner. Early dinner, easy food, shared in silence. Being with each other was enough.

One Sunday evening, the market hummed around them, the air sweet with roasted corn, vendors calling softly, shop lights blinking awake as twilight folded in. Meera's steps slowed when her eyes landed on a cushion—orange, bright like a small sun, patterned with wildflowers, caught in a stray beam of light.

Her fingers gently touched the fabric, as if feeling for a story. It was small, but in her mind, she saw it already on Aman's plain, grey couch, a splash of something soft and alive in the quiet room they were learning to share.

She set it down. "Just looking," she said to herself.

Aman, quiet beside her, picked it up again, turning it over like he was reading a new language. "You know," he said, "this would look good on the couch."

She blinked, caught off guard. "You don't have to—"

But he was already walking to the counter.

Pooja, close behind, nudged him with a grin. "See that? Meera's brightening your world, one cushion at a time."

Meera smiled, shaking her head. "I didn't want you to buy it. You don't have to change for me. I know bright colours aren't your thing."

He looked down at the cushion, then back at her, voice quiet but steady. “When someone is willing to change for another—because they want to, not because they’re made to—it’s not losing yourself. It’s just… a choice you make.” His fingers traced the edge of the fabric. “Maybe I’m starting to like bright colours.”

She looked at him, surprise fading into something quiet and steady. Her smile held a warmth that hadn’t been there before. Maybe it wasn’t just about the cushion. Maybe it was about letting a little colour in—into the room, into the day, into his life.

As they walked on, evening descended. Streetlights blinked awake, one by one. Meera glanced at Aman. There was something quieter in him now, an ease she hadn’t noticed before, a soft smile that stayed. Small, yes. But real.

And in that moment, she knew it wasn’t just the cushion that had changed things. It was him. Slowly. Deliberately. In ways neither of them had named yet.

Meera stepped off the train, and the air met her like memory—dust, marigolds, something sweet and fried drifting through it. Delhi wrapped around her in sound and scent. The station was loud, urgent, alive. But Diwali had softened its edges. Rickshaws blinked with fairy lights. Stalls spilled over with clay lamps, *kandils* swaying in the breeze, and boxes of sweets stacked in shiny paper like gifts waiting to be opened.

The city didn't just move, it sparkled.

By the time she reached home, the sky had turned the colour of pressed flowers, pink folding into gold. Her mother stood waiting at the door, brass *thali* in hand, the flame of the *diya* steady in the wind. She moved it in slow circles around Meera's face, lips moving in prayer. The scent of the *agarbatti* curled around them, quiet and warm. When her mother applied the red *tika* to her forehead, something inside Meera stilled, like she finally let go of a breath she hadn't realized she'd been holding.

Inside, Diwali was already there. A *rangoli* in bright pinks and greens stretched across the floor, smudged at the corners, imperfect, made with love. Lights clung to the walls, tangled but glowing. A cassette player crackled out an old *aarti*, its sound gentle, almost shy. On the dining table were trays of *kaju katli, gulab jamun, namak pare*, all lined up, ready for the neighbours, uncles, and kids from down the lane who came with sweets, stories, and noise.

Upstairs, the terrace wore rows of diyas like a necklace. Flames trembled in the evening wind. Somewhere, far off, firecrackers bloomed like slow flowers in the sky. Every house around them glowed, each a little world lit from within.

Baba bent near a flickering diya, shielding it with his hand. "Shri Ram is coming home tonight," he said, his voice low, steady, like always. Then, he began telling the story again: the long exile, the return, the rows of lamps lit across Ayodhya.

Meera listened, half-smiling. She knew every word, had heard it a hundred times. Still, she leaned in.

As a child, this was her favourite part of Diwali, more than the sweets, more than the sparklers. Just Baba's voice, slow and warm, making the world feel full of wonder again. She remembered sitting on the floor beside him, asking questions she already knew the answers to. And how he always answered anyway, like it was the first time.

Even now, something in her stilled. Not because of the light, the incense, or the celebration, but because of the story. And the way it sounded when it came from someone you loved.

She loved being home. The sweets, the diyas, the smell of ghee floating through warm rooms. Laughter rising like steam. But even as she smiled, something inside her leaned elsewhere.

Bangalore had slipped into her like a second skin, slow, unnoticed, fitting. Aman was in Kanpur, where the windows stayed unlit this Diwali. No boxes of sweets, no strings of marigolds or songs on tape. His father was gone and, with him, the celebration, too. But Aman still went home for Diwali. Not for the festival, not even for himself, but because sometimes, just being there, even in silence, says more than anything loud ever could. Presence, when nothing else is possible, becomes its own kind of prayer.

She pictured him in that house—dim kitchen, a single diya

flickering on the counter. Quiet hands making tea no one asked for. A silence too big to fill, yet too sacred to avoid.

She didn't miss Aman, not exactly. What she felt was not longing. It was softer than that. Like the after-smell of sparklers on skin, barely there, but still present. A trace that stayed long after the light had gone.

It was tenderness for him. For all the quiet load he held without telling. For the way he showed up, even when joy wasn't waiting.

Meera had chosen each gift like she was building a kind of prayer. Not grand, just precise. For Maa, a Mysore silk saree, deep red, like the *sindoor* tucked in the fold of her hairline, the fabric soft enough to carry memories. For Baba, a white kurta, simple, cotton, like the ones he wore on Sundays and festival mornings, still smelling faintly of sandalwood. And for Raju, the youngest and loudest, something new: a gaming console, packed with the latest Mario game, all bright colours and beeping joy. She could already see him disappearing into it for days.

When he tore through the wrapping, the plastic came off like a second skin. His eyes widened. "Wow! Thanks, Didi!" he shouted, hugging the box as if it had breath, as if joy came in wires and buttons.

She smiled at him, her grin easy, full.

Baba raised an eyebrow, something like a smirk tugging at the edge of his mouth. "A console? I thought maybe a few good books…"

The light in Raju's eyes dimmed, and the console was pulled slightly closer to his chest. But he blinked and stood a little taller. "I'll read too, Baba," he said, nodding like he was making a pact with himself, with all of them.

Baba sighed, not the heavy kind, not the kind that closed doors, but the kind that left windows open.

Meera reached for his arm, her fingers quiet on his sleeve. "Let him enjoy this," she said, voice steady. "Like you let me choose my way, he'll find his, too."

The moment passed but stayed, like the glow of a diya long after it's blown out, the warmth still hanging there, in the corners of the room.

The next morning, the house smelled of coconut oil and incense, like the promise of something about to begin. Meera sat cross-legged on the floor, her shawl slipping down one shoulder as Maa's fingers moved gently through her hair. The oil, warm and fragrant, soaked into her scalp as if trying to reach her thoughts.

Outside, the world was slowly waking. Inside, everything was still.

"Beta," Maa said, her voice light, almost offhand, "we should start looking for a suitable boy now. What do you say?"

Meera stilled. Her fingers paused in her lap.

"Maa, I just moved to Bangalore. Let me breathe there first."

Baba was sitting nearby, paper in hand, glasses low on his nose. He looked up, eyes steady. "Let her be," he said. "She's just begun writing her story. Don't turn the page too soon."

His words hung in the air, simple and soft. Meera looked at him, and in that quiet gaze, a thank you passed from her to him, wordless but full.

The rustle of newspaper returned. Maa's fingers resumed their rhythm. And though Meera didn't say his name aloud, though Aman was in another city and another kind of silence, the thought of him bloomed anyway. Maybe one day, he'll sit with me here. Maybe this oil, this morning, this peace—he'll belong to it, too.

That evening, the sky darkened without fanfare—*Amavasya*, the moon folding into itself. But inside the house, light took its place.

Diyas flickered on every windowsill, like soft breaths keeping the dark away. Maa moved like a poem in her red silk saree, the whisper of her *pallu* and the jingle of bangles trailing her like a memory. Baba lit incense sticks and set the *puja* thali in place with quiet reverence. Raju danced from room to room, too excited to stay still, already holding *phuljharis* like dreams waiting to unfold.

During Lakshmi Puja, time slowed. Hands were folded. Flowers were offered. Their voices rose together in a chant that felt like both tradition and tenderness. The marigolds, the ghee lamps, the scent of agarbattis—all of it clung to the walls, to their clothes, to the moment.

Afterwards, laughter returned like it had been waiting outside the door. Raju ran around with sparklers, his face brighter than the flames in his hand. Meera wrapped her shawl tighter and stood still, watching.

This Diwali was quiet, but full. Not grand, but whole. Raju's sparklers danced in the dark, and the sound of crackers echoed in the lane, but what stayed with her wasn't the noise. It was the way her family moved around each other, gently, teased, offered sweets, adjusted the wick of a diya without speaking. Even the silences had something to say.

She didn't realize it then, but the next Diwali wouldn't be the same. And maybe that was the gift—the not knowing. The way light shines brighter when you don't yet know it's about to dim. So, she stayed in the moment and let the laughter wrap around her, let the warmth of her mother's hand, her father's careful rituals, Raju's joy—all of it—sink into her bones.

Because right then, they were together. Whole. Unaware of the changes the next year would bring.

Later, when no one noticed, she stepped out into the courtyard. The peepal tree stood like a quiet witness. She looked up through its branches, then closed her eyes.

For a second, she could almost feel Aman there beside her, not in body but in memory, in feeling, watching Raju with her, watching the phuljharis arc through the night.

She placed her hand on the trunk and whispered, "Will my dreams come true? Will he ever be here with me?"

The tree didn't answer. It never did. But the breeze leaned in, almost listening. The air softened. And in that silence, Meera felt something say: Maybe.

The five days at home folded into each other like soft linen, creased with laughter, stained with turmeric and ghee.

Meera moved through them like someone waking into a dream, not quite ready to let it go.

But mornings come, and so do departures.

As she zipped her bag, the room felt smaller, the air heavier. Her mother hovered near the door, Baba standing behind with his arms folded, not saying much, but in their eyes was that familiar quiet question: Must you go so soon?

She hugged them both, lingering longer than usual, her fingers not wanting to let go.

Just as she turned to leave, Maa pressed a steel *dabba* into her hand, still warm from the stove. "For Pooja," she said gently. The lid clicked shut, sealing more care than words.

Meera nodded but didn't correct her. She didn't say that the *laddoos* were also for Aman. That he loved them the same way she did, biting into the softness, laughing when the coconut stuck to his teeth.

She held the box close, a small secret between her and the road ahead.

"Of course," she said, her voice light. "Pooja will love them."

The auto rickshaw moved through the familiar bends of Bangalore, past the corners she knew by smell and sound. Meera sat with her hands folded in her lap, heart beating a little faster with every turn. She thought of Aman, maybe leaning on the door frame, that small smile playing on his lips, the one that didn't need to try too hard.

She didn't expect fireworks. Not even arms wide open. Just... presence. A quiet hello. A look that said: You're back. Maybe chai, sweet and milky, the way she loved it, the way he never forgot.

But when she climbed the stairs, something tugged. The door was still locked. Doormat untouched. No shoes. No sound from inside. Only stillness.

Her fingers hesitated on the key. The air inside hadn't been touched in days. Curtains hung stiffly. The cushions were too perfect. It wasn't peace; it was something colder. A kind of waiting.

He'd said he'd be back yesterday.

She sat for a while, but the silence wasn't restful. It had edges. It scraped at her. She wrapped her dupatta around her, holding herself like a question she didn't want answered.

A few minutes later, she stepped out and walked to the corner STD booth. The paint was peeling off its frame, the glass smudged with fingerprints. Familiar in a way that felt grounding.

She dropped the coin in. The rotary dial turned slowly. Each number made a sound like a memory.

The phone rang.

Once. Twice.

Then came Pooja's voice, steady like always. "Meera? Everything okay?"

Meera breathed out. "I just reached. Aman's not here. I didn't know who else to call."

"He rang this morning," Pooja said. "His mother's unwell. He'll stay back a few more days. Come over. Stay with me till he's back."

Meera looked toward the apartment. The curtains hadn't moved. The shadows hadn't shifted. "It's okay," she said. "I'll stay here tonight. Just need to be still for a bit."

The street was cooling as she walked back. Evening folded into the city like a soft sheet. But the apartment didn't feel like home. Not yet. Not without him.

Later, after a plain meal, she tried to read, but the silence kept growing. Even the pages rustled too loudly. The room held its breath, and she held hers, too.

Just past midnight, Meera heard the door opening. A soft click. The kind that could mean anything… the wind, a mistake, or her mind, tired from waiting, filling in the sound. Her breath caught. Fear came first, fast. But behind it, quieter, something else: hope.

She sat up, her body stiff, listening.

Then: "Meera? It's me. Aman."

The voice was tired at the edges, but it was his.

She was on her feet before she knew it, the floor cold under her steps, her body rushing ahead of her mind. And there he was—the dust of travel on him, eyes tired but steady, lips pulling into the kind of smile that breaks things gently.

She went to him. No words. Just the space between them closing. Her arms around him, tight. Her face pressed against his chest, that familiar scent rising, sweat, road, and something like home.

"I'm sorry," he said. His voice was low, rough. "I didn't mean to scare you."

Meera didn't answer right away. She just held him closer, like answering with her body was easier. "I missed you," she whispered, not lifting her face.

"I missed you more," Aman said, one hand at the back of her head, fingers in her hair, like he was learning it again.

They pulled back, just slightly, and looked at each other, quiet, unblinking, their foreheads almost touching, eyes speaking in ways words never could.

Then slowly, like it wasn't the first time but still meant something, their lips met in a kiss, soft and steady, carrying the ache of every silence they had lived through. It was the kind of kiss that doesn't ask for anything, only answers what has always waited.

The room was dim, lit only by the soft orange glow of a streetlamp slipping through the curtains. A breeze moved gently through the mesh, shifting the air like a slow exhale. It smelled faintly of rain, of something just arrived or just leaving. But all Meera could feel was the steady rise and fall of Aman's chest beneath her fingers, a rhythm that didn't need words to prove he was there.

Later, they lay on the bed. No talk. Just breath. Just warmth.

Wrapped in each other like sleep, limbs tangled, breath syncing, the silence enveloping them like a second skin.

"I thought you'd be home when I got here," Meera said at last, her voice low, folding into the hush. "I opened the door… and when you weren't there, it felt like the room forgot how to breathe."

Aman turned slightly, just enough to find her hand in the dark. He laced his fingers through hers like a promise not spoken but understood. Then he lifted her hand and kissed each knuckle slowly, as if undoing every hour he had been late, every second she had sat alone in that hollow apartment.

"I should have been," he said. His words landed softly, like a coat laid gently across her shoulders. "You shouldn't have come back to an empty home. You should have walked straight into my arms."

They stayed like that, two stillnesses, uncertain but willing, learning how to meet in the silence. Breath in, breath out. Her forehead against his collarbone. His thumb tracing quiet circles on the inside of her wrist. The silence between them was no longer sharp but full, like soil, soft and ready.

Meera looked up at him, her eyes reading his. "You're here now," she said, steadier this time. "That's what matters."

Aman nodded. His eyes held the weight of softness, the kind that only comes after you've clenched your fists too long and finally learned to open them. He reached up and cupped her cheek.

"I'm not going anywhere," he said. "Not tonight. Not ever."

She let out a slow breath, like an answer. Like surrender.

Then she folded herself into him, one limb at a time, until she was stitched into his warmth. Her head rested on his chest, where the beat of his heart became a quiet song: looping, looping.

Outside, the streetlamp flickered once, then stilled. Tomorrow would come with its noise and need. But tonight, the world had shrunk to a bed, a breath, and a silence that no longer hurt.

A silence that finally made room for sleep, for return, for them.

Days folded into each other like bedsheets still warm from sleep. Not quite lovers, not just friends—they were becoming something else. Something that didn't need a name. A kind of gravity. A quiet orbit.

Mornings were slow and honey-coloured. Tea shared like a secret. Aman stealing bites from her toast without asking. Meera brushing past him in the kitchen, her fingers grazing his wrist like a sentence she didn't know how to finish.

Evenings arrived softly, dissolving into long hours on the floor or leaning against walls, talking in the half-light. Laughter like water over stones. Confessions that only made sense in the hush between midnight and dawn. Dreams that sounded braver in the dark.

At night, the world shrank to a bed just big enough for two. Whispered kisses. Sheets twisted like vines. Breath tangled with breath, as if they could slow down time by holding each other tightly enough.

It was never loud. Never grand. Love came softly. In the way Aman pulled the blanket over her without waking her. In the way Meera reached for his hand in her sleep, like a lighthouse to come back to.

They didn't speak the word. It felt too fragile, too loud for something so sacred. To name it would be to risk breaking it.

And Meera, watching this softer version of Aman unfold, this man who once seemed made only of silence and edges, could only wonder how much more he still held inside.

How some people open not with a bang, but like the first crack of light under a door.

At work, life wore its usual face.

Meera laughed with Pooja over lunch, passed sticky notes scribbled with inside jokes, and traded stories that filled the hours like background music.

But when it came to Aman, her mouth stayed closed.

Not out of secrecy or shame, but something gentler, more complicated, like holding a flame cupped in her palms, afraid the world might blow too hard.

Pooja had always known.

She had seen it in the pauses between Meera's sentences, the way his name settled on her tongue like something tasted, not just spoken.

She had teased, nudged, called it out years ago.

But wanting someone and finding yourself in their arms, folded into the ache of them, the familiarity of them, are two different oceans.

And swimming this close was not as easy as it looked.

Meera didn't speak of him, not because she was hiding, but because some loves aren't built for the noise. Because saying his name aloud might turn their silence into a shape too sharp to hold.

She wanted to live it before she explained it. To let it breathe in its own language.

How could she tell someone what it meant to wake up in his arms, to feel his breath like an answer against her skin?

How could she explain the way his gaze softened when it landed on her, like even her flaws were stories worth rereading?

Or the way they cooked, bumping elbows, burning the *rotis*, laughing at nothing.

How every evening ended in the same argument over which show to watch, only to fall asleep five minutes in, tangled and happy.

How do you describe a kind of love that asks for nothing but presence?

It wasn't fireworks. It was a slow, aching kind of silence. Like being chosen every day without ceremony. Like belonging, finally, in a body and a life that didn't ask her to shrink.

Pooja would've asked a hundred questions: When did it start? What does it mean? Is it serious?

And Meera, who once told Pooja everything, now held this one thing like a pressed flower between the pages of her heart.

Too fragile. Too sacred. Too hers.

For now, the silence was not a wall, but a garden.

Something still growing. Something not yet ready for the world's eyes.

It was real. And it was enough.

The weeks passed like warm water, shapeless, slow, slipping between their fingers without resistance.

Pooja hadn't been around much. Last Sunday was busy with her sister's baby shower, a quiet celebration full of hope and gentle excitement.

Meera missed her, but softly, like missing a familiar streetlight on a quiet walk. And yet, she didn't mind the stillness. It gave her space to feel this new shape between her and Aman, not yet a story, not yet named, just breath, body, and being.

But this Sunday… something tilted.

The city moved slower than usual, as if the streets themselves had rolled back under a blanket. No plans. No signs. Just air, quiet and waiting.

Pooja didn't think twice. It was just a whim. She thought of surprising them. A flicker of impulse, a laugh under her breath. And so she did.

She arrived early. The street outside Aman's place was still wrapped in dream-light. She pressed the doorbell, soft but sure, and waited with a smile curled at the corners of her mouth.

Inside, Aman stirred, the bell folding into his half-sleep. Meera lay against him, her breath rising and falling, the way small boats move with the tide. He moved gently, like leaving something sacred. He peeled himself from the shape of her sleep and padded to the door, bones still heavy with warmth. He opened it, blinking. "Pooja?" he said, voice rough at the edges. "It's early…"

"Surprise!" she grinned. Her voice held that old mischief, the kind that always arrived just before the questions. "I missed our Sunday rituals. Couldn't stay away." She stepped in like she'd always belonged to the place.

Aman rubbed his eyes. "Meera's still asleep," he murmured.

"Of course," she smirked. "Lazy Sundays. All of us." Her gaze sparkled, catching on the silence. "Guess I'll go wake her."

Aman didn't stop her. Just shrugged, the universal language of 'I don't know how to say this yet'.

Pooja padded down the hallway and turned toward Meera's room. Empty. She froze, her brow arched. "Wait. You said she was sleeping…"

Aman, caught mid-exhale, pointed with one hand. Not forward. To the side.

Pooja's eyes followed the gesture. His room. She looked back at him, eyes wide. "There?"

Aman's silence was a confession, his neck colouring faintly with the truth.

Pooja's grin grew wide. "You mean… she's in your bed?"

He nodded once, a small gesture, but it held an ocean.

She tiptoed forward, curiosity lifting her like wind. At the door, she pushed just enough.

Inside, Meera lay curled in the centre of the bed, her hair like a river spilled across the pillow, one arm tucked beneath her cheek.

The sheets around her told stories without language—folds, creases, warmth still lingering. The bed held two absences, but only one presence.

Pooja turned, her mouth open in mock shock, a hand to her heart.

"You said she was sleeping," she whispered, eyes glittering. "You didn't say she was sleeping here."

Aman looked everywhere but at her. The back of his neck turned pink.

She leaned in, voice low with teasing reverence, like naming something holy.

"This isn't Sunday brunch," she said. "This is Sunday…full package, *yaar*." Just then, from under the covers, Meera let out a sound, something between a sigh and a groan, like a note escaping a dream. She opened one eye slowly, as if the morning was still deciding whether to arrive, and when she saw Pooja at the door, both eyes sprang open, startled, bright.

Then, like a wave folding back into the sea, she vanished, the blanket swallowing her whole, a pillow dragged over her head like armour.

Her voice, muffled, reached out from under the fabric: "I swear I was going to tell you… just… not like this."

Aman laughed softly, raking a hand through his hair. "I'll make tea and breakfast," he said, stepping away, a soldier retreating from a battlefield that hadn't declared war yet.

In the kitchen, the pan began to murmur. The air grew fragrant with cardamom and ginger, the old language of comfort. Aman moved through the motions with memory more than thought, the way a hand remembers music after years. He wasn't listening. But he wasn't not listening either.

Pooja's voice floated in first, full of mischief, teasing, light like wind through beads.

"Meera," she said, her tone dipped in sugar, "have you told him yet? That your heart was his the minute he walked into that classroom, that you've been in love with him since college?"

From beneath the blanket came a moan, somewhere between protest and surrender. "Not yet..."

In the kitchen, Aman stirred the tea as if stirring the moment itself. And he remembered. The first day. That still frame lodged in the heart's quiet corners.

She had walked in, clutching a notebook like it might shield her from the world. Eyes wide, searching. She took the window seat, sunlight combing her hair like it was familiar with her. And that was it. She didn't try to stand out; she just did.

When class ended, his feet moved before permission could be asked.

"Meera," he'd called.

She turned, startled, like someone who'd heard their name spoken in a dream.

He could've asked anyone, really.

"Where's the library?"

She blinked, then smiled, unsure. "The place with all the books?"

It should've been silly. But something in him softened. From her, it wasn't a joke. It was music, a note too honest to question.

Later that day, he saw her again, beneath the old peepal tree, cross-legged beside Pooja, book open like a doorway. Her hair kept falling on her face. She didn't fix it. She just let the breeze decide. A pale pink salwar, the white dupatta slipping off her shoulder like it belonged more to the wind than to her. She wasn't doing anything. She was just… there. Reading. Laughing. Breathing.

And somehow, that was enough.

He meant to walk past. He really did. But his body paused, the way the tide pauses at the shore, waiting.

There, under the sway of leaves and light, something inside him adjusted quietly, like a painting straightened on a wall.

Love didn't arrive like thunder. It came like that—a girl laughing under a tree and a boy who didn't yet know that some beginnings don't introduce themselves. They just are.

Aman smiled, lifting the cups onto the tray, each clink landing softly in the silence. Then he walked back. Back to the room. Back to the moment that had taken root all those years ago, unnoticed, like seeds that bloom without witness.

What he didn't know then was that Meera had always loved him. Quietly. Like a secret folded into a prayer. And maybe, just maybe, this time, it was ready to be said aloud.

The weeks slipped by like silk through fingers, soft, unnoticed, and suddenly gone. Bangalore's winter wasn't cruel like Delhi's; it was a gentler chill that kissed the bones rather than bite them. The kind of cold that asked for the comfort of old socks, steaming cups of *adrak* chai, and the hush of two bodies learning the shape of each other beneath a blanket.

The city whispered in lights. Rooftops wore fairy dust in the form of bulbs. The scent of roasted peanuts spiralled through narrow lanes like memory, and somewhere, always somewhere, a boy with a guitar strummed the ache of someone else's heart into the wind.

New Year's Eve came quietly, then all at once.

Bangalore pulsed like a heartbeat turned outward, laughter spilling out of restaurant doors, fireworks bursting like questions no one had answers to, people dancing not just with each other but against the weight of another year passed.

Meera had called Maa and Baba earlier that day. She told them she was with friends and left it at that. Didn't say "club". Didn't say "midnight". Didn't say "Aman".

She could still hear Maa's worry echoing in her head: "It's not safe for girls to be out so late, Meera. What will people say?"

Girls like her weren't raised for nights like these. They were handed recipes, routines, and rules, not the trembling freedom of unscripted hours. For someone from a middle-class, dutiful, tightly scripted life, there were only so many pages you were allowed to turn. And even fewer you were ever allowed to write yourself.

Sometimes she missed the small rituals of home. The newspaper unfolding like a map in Baba's hands. Maa's footsteps, always heading toward the kitchen, always toward care disguised as rice and dal. Everything known. Everything named.

That life wasn't lost. It was just quieter now. Folded, like a letter in her pocket.

But this was hers, too. A different street. A different girl. Or maybe just the same girl, unbraided. Becoming not new, but more.

Maybe Maa and Baba wouldn't understand.

Maybe they couldn't.

But maybe, just maybe, they felt it—the slow tremble of the world changing and their daughter moving with it.

She stood in the blur of light and sound, lifted her glass, and clinked it against Aman's, then Pooja's.

The tequila went down like a dare, fire shaped like water.

Her first.

Even Aman, who usually drank silence and sunlight, laughed with his whole chest tonight, like someone who had finally forgiven something inside himself.

Pooja's fingers found hers, warm, reckless, and tugged her into the beat.

Meera didn't resist.

She danced, not to be seen, but to be let go of. She laughed like forgiveness. She lived like someone trying joy on for the first time.

The lights spun above her like questions she no longer needed to answer. The floor tilted, caught her, let her go again. And Aman's eyes, steady, sure, found her through it all.

Something changed that night. Or maybe it simply revealed what was already waiting.

She wasn't someone else. She was just, finally, fully, freely, herself.

Not because of the drink. Not because the music carried her.

But because she chose every step, every laugh, every wild heartbeat. Because, for once, she wasn't asking if it was right or wrong.

She was just living. And that, too, was a kind of becoming.

By the time they reached the apartment, Meera's head was swaying, not from the drink alone, but from the afterglow of something larger.

The night still clung to her skin: music like a second heartbeat, laughter echoing in her bones, a strange, sudden lightness as if she'd stepped out of her own shadow.

She turned to Aman. Her eyes weren't asking anymore.

They were saying: I know now.

A spark lived there, not new, just finally visible.

Before he could speak, she crossed the distance between them. Her lips met his, certain, deliberate.

No more waiting. No more weighing what was allowed. Not tonight.

Aman froze, breath caught, then let go. He smiled into the kiss, like someone recognizing home. His hands moved up her back, patient and warm, and Meera trembled, not with fear, but with the recognition of being seen.

Completely.

This wasn't about heat. It was something quieter, older, like language that didn't need sound. It folded around them like dusk, soft, full of knowing.

It was different. It was them, unhidden.

For the first time, she saw something shift in Aman's eyes, not just love but understanding. Not the kind that explains but the kind that stays.

He didn't try to capture her or reach for possession. He just was, steady, present, enough.

And in that silence between two people who no longer needed to ask permission, Meera felt herself settle, like water finding the curve of its shore.

Later, wrapped in the hush of their warmth, her breath slowed.

She had known Aman's touch before, but tonight, she touched his truth. And he touched hers.

This was a man she could grow old beside.

She would wait a lifetime if it led her there.

When dawn spilled its first colours into the sky—blush and gold like soft promises—Meera woke in his arms.

Safe.

Held.

Sure.

Not forever. But of this beginning. And how much she didn't want to lose it.

But the world, she would learn, has a way of rearranging what we think we've just begun.

"Auntie will be fine," Pooja said, her voice gentle. "It's just a fever. They're doing tests. She'll feel better the moment she sees you."

Meera nodded. The motion felt practised.

She had told the lie so many times it had started to feel like a second skin. Not quite hers, but close enough to pass.

Aman adjusted the strap of her bag across his shoulder, his fingers trembling at the edges. The way light trembles before rain.

"Are you sure you don't want me to come with you? It's really no problem, Meera."

She shook her head, too fast, too sharply, like pulling a thread that might unravel everything. "No," she said, her voice almost steady. "It's just a few days. You have your studies. Please... stay focused."

He exhaled slowly, the kind of breath that wanted to say more but didn't know how to carry the weight of it.

Maybe he already knew. Maybe somewhere inside him, something had already begun to loosen, the way leaves let go in October, not because they want to, but because something inside says it's time.

The loudspeaker sliced through the silence, a voice without a face, announcing the train like a priest calls the name of the dead.

Clear. Final.

Echoing in the hollow of her chest like a coin dropped deep in water.

This goodbye wasn't just a goodbye.

It was an ending.

When the time came to board, Meera turned to Aman. She didn't care who saw them. She kissed him. Softly at first. A brush of lips, hesitant, tender, aching.

Then deeper.

Like she wanted to press the moment into her skin, to hold on one last time.

Aman froze, startled.

But then he kissed her back, arms wrapping tightly around her. He didn't pull away. He didn't ask. He just held her, like he knew exactly what this meant. His hands pressed the small of her back, steadying, anchoring, grounding her.

She'd never done this before. Not in public. Not like this. Not with all the world watching.

She let herself fall into it. The taste of him on her lips. The way his fingers curled along her spine, like they were holding on to her whole body. The way he sighed into her mouth, like she was the only thing left in the world.

When she finally pulled back, her chest ached, her lips still tingled with him. Aman's eyes searched hers, his brows tight with worry, holding a question that words couldn't reach.

"Meera," he said softly, "is your mother really okay? Are you telling me everything?"

She forced a smile, her best one, practised and perfect. "She's sick, but she'll be fine. You don't need to worry."

But behind her back, her hand slipped up, crossing fingers—a secret habit, a quiet lie.

Her father's voice echoed in her mind: If a lie is meant to protect, is it really a lie at all?

She held that thought tight, trying to quieten the guilt pressing heavily against her ribs.

"I can come with you," Aman said again, almost pleading.

She shook her head. "No. That'll just make things harder. She's already stressed. I'll be okay."

He didn't argue, but his eyes stayed on her, searching, asking questions she wasn't ready to answer. She turned away before he could say more. She stepped onto the train and gripped the cold metal bar to steady herself.

The train whistle blew, sharp, final.

Aman stepped forward, like he wanted to call her back, but stopped.

She smiled through the ache in her chest and waved until her arm burned.

The platform blurred. Aman and Pooja were left behind, their faces frozen in her mind like a photograph.

It began on a day so painfully ordinary that it might have dissolved into memory without leaving a trace, a day filled with the humdrum sounds of office life: the shuffle of files, the soft scratch of pens moving across paper, the repetitive whirring of a ceiling fan that had long forgotten to rest. Meera had gone through the motions, breathing, working, existing, like someone ticking boxes on a list she hadn't written.

Pooja wasn't around. Her sister had just delivered a baby, and the photo she sent of tiny, wrinkled toes and a sleeping face scrunched in newborn fatigue brought a momentary smile to Meera's lips. The desk beside her stood still but not empty; it held the residue of Pooja's presence—an uncapped pen, a half-filled notebook with an idea jotted down for the next article: "Women Who Leave, And Why."

The day trudged along, unremarkable. Outside the office, a peon poured tea into steel tumblers with the practised grace of routine. Inside, the low murmur of conversations and laughter rose and fell, never too loud, never too still, like a song everyone half-remembered.

And then, without warning, the world tilted.

It happened twice that day. A sudden dizziness crept behind her eyes like a tide swelling without notice. Her hands clutched the edge of the desk as a wave of nausea threatened to overwhelm her. She told herself it was nothing—maybe she hadn't eaten enough, maybe she had slept too little. But even the shadows in the corners of the room began to feel strange, pulsing unnaturally.

When the same thing happened the next morning, only sharper, stronger, more aggressive, a silence opened inside her, deep and echoing. It was the kind of silence that doesn't ask questions but plants one anyway.

*What if I'm pregnant?*

She didn't recoil from the thought. It wasn't fear—not in the way people spoke of it—of motherhood, not when it was Aman. In fact, something about the idea was quietly beautiful, like pressing your hand to a bakery window in winter and feeling the warmth inside, knowing you can't enter, but still wanting to stay close.

But she also knew the timing was all wrong. Not like this. Not now. Not while unmarried. Not when her parents' trust sat on her shoulders like an heirloom coat, borrowed, cherished, and never to be stained.

She went to the hospital. The place smelled of disinfectant, but beneath it lingered something older—fear, perhaps. The waiting room was filled with people pretending not to look at one another. A nurse called her name. The doctor was kind and efficient, asking for blood tests and scans "just to be thorough."

She nodded, tucking her nervousness into a polite smile, a smile so tight it felt like folding a letter she never wanted anyone to read.

The next day, she returned to collect her reports, thinking it would be over in a few minutes. But the receptionist looked at the file, then at Meera, and paused. "Dr Subramanyam would like to speak with you," she said, with a tone that suddenly felt too careful.

In that moment, time didn't stop, but Meera did. Her body froze between faded health posters and rows of plastic chairs. Her heart didn't race; it braced, as if already preparing for a truth it had sensed before her mind had caught up.

Inside the doctor's room, the air felt denser, more deliberate. Dr Subramanyam sat across from her, his words cautious, like he was walking barefoot on glass.

"There's something in your blood work," he said. "And the scan shows an area we need to understand better."

He paused, then added, "We'll need to do a biopsy."

Meera didn't ask anything. She didn't argue. She didn't cry. She just sat there, nodding slowly, her eyes fixed on a crack in the wall behind him.

Biopsy.

She hadn't even heard the word clearly, but the sound of it dropped into her chest like lead. It didn't matter whether she understood it in medical terms. Something in her did. Something ancient and intuitive.

She walked out of the hospital like a half-erased sketch, her form intact, but the definition gone.

She didn't tell Aman or Pooja.

It wasn't about not trusting them; it was about her own voice. She knew it would tremble. And once you say something aloud, it grows teeth. She wasn't ready for what the truth might unravel.

Pooja was busy with her sister's new baby, with bottles, lullabies, and a life that had just begun. Meera didn't want to break that bubble.

And Aman… she couldn't tell him. Not yet.

Not because she didn't love him.

But maybe because she did.

She remembered the way his face changed when his father passed, the quiet ache behind his eyes, how he held himself together like a house with too many cracks, how silence wrapped around him, thicker than anything she could say.

She remembered the dreams he let go of, how he spoke less after that, how even his laughter felt careful, like it might break if it got too loud.

She couldn't hand him this, not when he had only just begun to breathe easy again. Not when she still had the strength to carry it herself.

It wasn't that she didn't trust him.

It was that she wasn't ready for what her truth might do to him.

Sometimes silence isn't distance.

Sometimes it's protection.

The word 'cancer' was never spoken. But it hung in the room, in the way the nurse looked away, in the stillness of the doctor's hands.

The biopsy confirmed what her body already feared. It wasn't benign. It wasn't still. It was moving, spreading, like ink dropped into water.

"You'll need immediate treatment," the doctor said. "We have to act quickly."

Meera, ever composed, simply asked, "Can you refer me to someone in Delhi?"

Because Bangalore had grown too small for secrets. Because distance, she thought, might make her brave.

The doctor scribbled down a name—Dr Sharma—and handed the paper to her like a boarding pass.

"You'll need support," he said gently. "Your family—"

"I know," Meera replied. This time, her voice didn't shake.

She told Aman her mother was unwell—"just a fever"—and that she needed to go home for a few days. When she smiled, it wasn't just a lie; it was a plea: Please believe me. Please don't ask questions I can't answer.

When she kissed him goodbye at the station, it wasn't just a kiss. It was something more final. A sealing of memory. A pressing of skin to skin, as if to say: Hold this version of me. The one before.

On the train, the world moved past the window in a blur. Meera sat still, holding the armrest like it was the only solid thing left.

Inside her, the silence grew.

This was the only way.

Even if it meant breaking. Even if it meant disappearing without explanation.

Because sometimes, love does not declare itself with grand gestures. Sometimes, it walks away, barefoot, bleeding, just to spare the one it loves from having to watch it fall.

Meera came home quietly, not like a daughter returning with laughter and stories, but more like a shadow slipping in at twilight, unnoticed but present. There was no grand announcement, no dramatic entrance. Just the hush of familiar footsteps echoing in the hallway. It was the kind of silence that doesn't demand attention because it already knows the weight of what's unspoken.

Her mother welcomed her at the door with a slow aarti, a small flame circling her daughter's face, and a red tilak pressed gently on her forehead. It felt more like a protective seal than a ritual, as if trying to ward off something unseen but deeply felt. Meera didn't flinch, but she noticed the slight tremble in her mother's fingers, how they lingered just a second longer, as if hoping to read her pain through touch alone.

Her father lowered the newspaper, not with surprise, but with concern etched into his features, the kind softened by time, born from knowing someone deeply and sensing when they are carrying more than they say.

Raju came running. He threw himself into her arms like he had been waiting to catch a star that had fallen from the sky. His hug was warm, honest, and uncomplicated.

In that moment, she almost believed she could be whole again.

They surrounded her with love, wrapped her in it like a familiar shawl. It should have felt comforting. Instead, it felt like a weight, gentle but heavy.

Love can be like that sometimes.

"You're hiding something," her mother said softly, studying her face. There was no anger in her voice, just a quiet ache.

Meera smiled softly. "I just missed home… and your aloo parathas." It was the kind of lie that sounds harmless but carries the burden of a thousand truths left unsaid.

The house fell quiet again. Not an uncomfortable silence but one that holds space for things that cannot yet be voiced.

Maybe she would tell them tomorrow, but not tonight. Not while their eyes still held hope for ordinary mornings.

That night, as she lay under the old ceiling fan, it felt like the ceiling itself had turned into the sky. She listened to her parents' conversation through the thin walls. She closed her eyes and thought: *Just one more night of peace, even if it's borrowed, even if it's a pretence.*

Because how does a daughter say, "I am not okay," in a way that doesn't break the very people who raised her? How do you name the fear that has already arrived, the one that wears your own face in the mirror?

But by morning, she knew she couldn't carry it alone.

The morning unfolded as it always did. The birds called from the peepal tree. The smell of incense drifted through the house. Her father read the paper with his usual seriousness.

But inside Meera, something had fractured.

She rose early, not out of routine, but with purpose. Maa stood in the kitchen, making tea. The spoon clinked gently against the glass, rhythmic, familiar.

She could have called Baba in right then, could have said it over the steam rising between them.

But she didn't want to say it there, not with the clatter of cups, not with the scent of cardamom and routine, not in a room that held too much of everything unsaid.

She didn't want to say it inside the house, with its quiet demands, its walls heavy with knowing, its silences louder than words.

So, she stepped outside to the peepal tree.

Its branches had known her secrets.

It had held her sobs.

It had caught her wishes, when they were still too small to fly.

Raju played nearby, laughing at something. The innocence of that sound gave her courage. She turned to her parents, who had followed her out, and said, "There's something I need to tell you."

Her voice was steady, but her hands were cold.

They looked at her, not with suspicion, but with quiet waiting, the kind of stillness that only love can hold.

"I'll be staying home for a while," Meera said. "There's some treatment I need to undergo."

Her mother paused, holding the teacup mid-air. "Treatment?" she asked carefully.

Meera nodded. "It's early. It's manageable. I've already seen a doctor in Bangalore."

The word she hadn't yet said was already floating in the air between them.

Her father asked, "What kind of treatment?"

She inhaled deeply.

"Chemotherapy," she replied, as softly as one might confess to something fragile.

Her mother blinked hard. "Chemo?" she repeated, as if testing the word's weight on her tongue. Then, after a beat, she added, "Why?"

But she already knew the answer. She just didn't want to hear it aloud.

Meera nodded again. "Yes. It's cancer. Stage 2. It has been caught early. The prognosis is good."

Her mother reached out instinctively, placing her hand on Meera's lips. "Don't say that," she whispered. "Don't say that word."

She pulled her hand back slowly, as if the truth had burned her.

"I didn't know how to tell you," Meera said. "I didn't want to scare you."

Her father was quiet for a long moment. Then he said, gently but firmly, "You're not alone in this."

Meera looked at the ground. Then at him.

"I don't want Raju to know. Not yet."

Her mother nodded.

"No," she said. "Let's not give him this to carry."

Her father asked, "When do the sessions begin?"

"Next week."

"We'll go with you," her mother said.

Meera tried to protest. "You really don't have to."

But her father cut in, "We want to. That's final."

"You don't have to do this alone," her mother added, her voice cracking just a little.

Baba's voice was softer this time.

"What else is a family for?"

Meera didn't argue. She couldn't.

She only whispered, "Okay."

Nothing else was said.

The birds sang louder above them, as if trying to fill the space that words could not.

And in that moment, something inside her softened. The truth had landed. And though it hurt, she no longer carried it alone.

They were in it now, together.

The battle had begun.

The first round of chemotherapy was over, but the war was far from won.

Meera sat on the hospital bed, an IV line snaking from her wrist, feeding a slow, measured dose into her veins. The needle had slid in with a slight prick, and now the cool solution crept up her arm, spreading a cold heaviness inside her. The room reeked of antiseptic and something colder. Sterile. Unfeeling. As the bag above her slowly emptied, the reality of the treatment settled in, quiet but undeniable.

The first few minutes had been manageable. Then the nausea crept in, subtle at first, like a whisper in her gut. Then, like an oncoming storm, it built up, wave after wave, relentless. She squeezed her eyes shut, breathing deeply, willing herself to stay still. But her body had other plans.

The nurse handed her a small basin just in time. "It gets worse before it gets better," she murmured kindly, rubbing her back. "Just breathe."

Meera had read about this. Chemotherapy didn't discriminate. It attacked everything—the good, the bad, all of it. It left her drained, hollowed out.

By the third session, the changes began.

At first, it was subtle strands of her thick, dark hair left behind on her scarf, a few more tangled in her brush. She ignored it. Pretended not to notice. But soon, the strands slipped away like grains of sand, gathering silently in her hands.

The treatments were done in daycare. She'd go in the morning and return by evening. Sometimes Maa accompanied her, sometimes Rekha Bua. Maa tried to come every time, but Meera insisted she rest. "You'll wear yourself out, Maa. It's just a few hours. Bua will come today." Reluctantly, Maa agreed.

That evening, after Bua dropped her off at home, Meera sat on her bed and picked up the small mirror from her bedside table. The face staring back was still hers—tired eyes, familiar jawline—but she knew that wouldn't last. She ran her hand through her hair. More strands came loose, slipping through her fingers like forgotten promises.

Aman had always loved her hair. He would play with it absentmindedly as they talked, letting the strands drift through his fingers.

"It's so soft," he'd murmur. "Like silk." She'd roll her eyes, pretending his words didn't make her heart race. Now there was nothing left to twirl. Nothing for him to love. But this, at least, would grow back. She had lost more than hair.

She had lost Aman and Pooja. She hadn't spoken to either of them in days. Pooja's calls had stopped. The silence between them was now louder than the words they hadn't said.

And somewhere, in the silence between hospital visits and sleepless nights, she had lost a part of herself too, a part she wasn't sure she could ever reclaim.

At first, Pooja had called regularly, her voice laced with worry. "You're still in Delhi? What's going on, Meera?"

Meera stuck to the lie she had begun. "Maa's not keeping well," she'd say. "The doctor suspects typhoid. I'm staying back to help her recover."

Each time, the words felt heavier on her tongue, but they were safer than the truth.

Pooja didn't sound convinced. "Aman's been asking about you. He's worried."

Meera hesitated, then replied gently, "Tell him not to worry, okay? He needs to focus. He must crack that civil services exam. It is his dream. Just… tell him I'll write to him soon. Once things settle here, I'll be back in Bangalore."

Cancer wasn't just a disease of the body; it was a war of the spirit, a battle that chipped away at everything familiar, everything safe.

She hadn't just lost weight. She had lost certainty, control, the quiet trust that her body would carry her through a day without betraying her.

Each morning, she had to remind herself why she was still fighting. Some days, she couldn't find the answer.

She'd seen what this illness brought with it—careers halted, school years suspended, childhoods put on hold. She'd seen the empty chairs, the silent corridors, the families who walked in together and left one short.

And all the while, outside the hospital walls, the world kept turning. Cars honked. Cafés buzzed with laughter. Friends planned weekend getaways. Families celebrated birthdays. Life didn't pause, not for illness. Not even for grief.

But her world had shrunk. To IV poles. To appointments on calendars. To tired sighs and the rustle of hospital gowns.

And that was the cruellest part.

Cancer didn't just take.

It stripped. It erased. And sometimes, it gave nothing back.

She wasn't sure she'd ever find her way back to the girl who used to laugh without glancing over her shoulder. The one who planned for tomorrow without fearing what it might bring.

Pooja's calls had now stopped.

It had begun with her resignation.

She remembered the moment—sitting at her desk, head spinning, body failing her. She stared at the blank screen of her laptop, the room blurring around the edges.

And then, with cold, exhausted clarity, she realized the organization wouldn't slow down for her. And neither would life.

She didn't want to quit, but she had to.

She sent the email, then waited in silence until the phone rang.

It was Pooja.

"Meera, what is this? You've resigned? You've disappeared. What's going on?"

Meera had closed her eyes. The moment had come. "I'm getting married."

A pause. Sharp. Confused.

"What? Getting married? To whom?"

"My parents found someone. He's a civil servant. Well-settled. Maa hasn't been well… they think it's time."

Another silence. Then disbelief.

"Meera, are you hearing yourself? What about Aman? You love him. If something's wrong, tell me. I'll come to Delhi. We'll fix it."

Meera swallowed hard. "I can't say no to them, Pooja. Not now. Not after everything. They think this will bring stability. And he's… he's a good man."

The lie tasted bitter.

Pooja's voice dropped. Tight. Wounded.

"Stability? That's what you call it? You're walking away from everything—your job, your dreams, Aman—and pretending this is normal?"

"Please," Meera whispered. "Just make sure he stays focused on his exam. That's all I ask."

Pooja was silent. Then, her voice cracked in a way Meera hadn't heard before. "You know what hurts the most? That you didn't trust me enough to tell me the truth. You're not the Meera I knew."

And just like that, the line went dead.

Since that night, Pooja hadn't called. As expected, she had told Aman.

Meera knew he'd call. He never had before, but some truths are too loud to stay hidden. What she hadn't expected was that it would happen so soon.

The very next evening, the phone rang.

Aman's voice cracked through the line, raw and aching. "Meera... please tell me this is a joke."

"It's not," she said quietly.

"I'm coming to Delhi."

She hesitated, heart pounding, then replied with forced calm, "Fine. Meet me at Connaught Place."

She hadn't wanted him to see her, not like this. The truth had started showing on her face. Her skin had dulled, the weight loss was no longer just a number on a scale, and her scarf now covered more than modesty.

She had layered on makeup that morning—concealer beneath tired eyes, a soft shade on her lips. She'd rehearsed her lines, tucked every loose strand under her scarf.

But she knew she couldn't truly hide what was happening.

Still, she went.

Because Aman deserved a goodbye. A closure. Even if she couldn't give him the truth.

She saw him before he saw her, standing near the fountain, scanning the crowd.

When their eyes met, his face softened, then darkened with worry. His steps quickened.

"You've lost weight," Aman said, his voice low, laced with concern.

Meera adjusted the scarf over her head, pulling it tighter, as though it could shield her from what was coming.

"I'm preparing for my wedding. My fiancé likes lean girls."

Aman flinched. His eyes scanned her face, searching for truth, for doubt, for her. "You're changing yourself for him?"

Meera didn't flinch. She met his gaze, steady and calm. "Yes, I am."

Aman looked stunned. But before he could speak, she continued, her voice quiet but firm.

"Don't you remember what you once told me? That change isn't wrong…that when one chooses to change for someone, there's no harm in it. You said that to me, Aman. And I believed you." Her voice wavered slightly, but she didn't stop. "I'm not being forced to change. I want to. This is my decision."

Aman's expression twisted in disbelief and pain. "Why are you choosing him over me?"

Her breath caught, but she forced her face to remain still. "Why not?" she said, the words falling too easily, like a rehearsed line from a play.

"He offers stability. A home. A respectable family. My father's happy. Why would I choose uncertainty when everything I need is right here?" She paused, and then, quietly, almost as if to herself, she added, "It's not certain you'll clear the exam, Aman. How long could

I keep waiting? How long could I keep dreaming about a future that may never come?"

Aman's hands curled into fists, his eyes blazing. "So…everything we had meant nothing to you?"

Meera held his gaze, even as her heart thudded in her chest. Every word she'd spoken was a lie, but one she had forced herself to believe. *You can't know the truth, Aman.*

She swallowed the lump in her throat and offered a smile, small, hollow, breaking at the edges. "It was good while it lasted."

Aman looked at her one last time. Then turned away.

No words. No parting line. Just silence and the sound of footsteps growing fainter with each step.

She watched him walk away.

Every instinct screamed at her to call out, to run after him, to pull him back into her arms. But she stood still. The scarf clung tighter to her scalp as the wind picked up and her fingers curled around its edge, holding it down, like a tether to the life she was pretending to choose.

She waited until he had disappeared around the corner before letting herself collapse onto the nearest bench.

Only then did she allow the mask to fall.

Her chest heaved, and tears spilled quietly down her cheeks, not the kind that demanded attention, but the kind that came from somewhere deep and hollow.

In that moment, she wasn't the brave daughter, the graceful patient, or the girl who had made a sensible choice.

She was just Meera.

A girl trying to survive.

A girl who had just let go of the only person who made her feel whole.

That night, Meera sat by the window, the peepal tree outside casting long shadows in the moonlight. It had stood there before she was born, its roots deep, its branches wide, sheltering everyone beneath.

But she wasn't like the tree. Not yet.

And somewhere deep inside, she knew Aman wouldn't let this be the end. Not because of what they had lost but because of what he still needed to prove.

Maybe that was the real goodbye she had given him. Not a parting, but a challenge. And maybe, just maybe, in letting go, she had given Aman the one thing he still needed most—a reason to rise. A reason to become the future she no longer felt worthy of.

She turned away from the window and reached for the leather-bound diary her father had once gifted her. The pages felt heavier than usual tonight.

She began to write.

Dear Aman,

I will never send you this letter, but I need to write it because if I don't, I might break.

When I told you I was getting married, I saw the way your eyes darkened, the way your body stiffened, as if I had stolen something from you. And I did, didn't I? I stole our future. I crushed the dreams we built together. But you will never know why.

You will never know that the woman you loved is no longer the same. That she is standing at the edge of a battle she never saw coming. That she is terrified.

But I could not let you fight this war beside me.

You would have stayed. You would have held my hand through every painful treatment. You would have given up your dreams just to make sure I survived. And I couldn't allow that. I love you too much to let you break with me.

So, I chose cruelty. I made you hate me because hate is easier to survive than helplessness. If I had told you the truth, you would have never left.

Aman, my love…you must move forward. You must forget me. You must live. And if I survive this battle, if I make it to the other side, perhaps in another lifetime, I will find you again.

Until then,<br>
Meera

Meera sat on her bed, the blanket tucked around her waist. The room held its breath. Outside, the world moved in small, steady ways—the creak of a gate, the whistle of a pressure cooker, the slow hum of the fan overhead.

That morning, she had heard the words she had never let herself say aloud:

"You're cancer-free."

She had hoped, yes, but gently, like someone walking across thin ice. For months, she had lived between prayers and possibilities, careful not to let one cancel the other. And then, just like that, the doctor had spoken these words, with a calm voice and soft eyes, words that rang through her louder than anything since the day cancer had first entered her life.

But it was only now, as evening light slipped past the curtains and the house stilled again, that the words began to settle inside her. Not just the relief but everything else. The weight of it. The year she had lived through.

Beside her lay the file, thin, almost careless in its size. But inside it: A year of storms. White hospital walls. Sharp needles. Machines that beeped without mercy. Murmured prayers. And a fear that had become part of her breath.

Almost a year had passed since she'd left Bangalore and come home for treatment. The days since had blurred into hospital visits, long afternoons in bed, and nights that stretched too far.

Summer came. The rains followed. Festivals passed, unnoticed.

She had stayed indoors, quietly fighting, while the world outside kept turning.

Her mind drifted to three months ago—Diwali, once her favourite time of year. But this time, it didn't feel like Diwali at all. The house had been quiet. No fairy lights. No crackers.

Maa had prepared sweets, but didn't taste them. Baba, who usually filled the house with stories and *shlokas*, had nothing to say. Even Raju, once wild with excitement, sat beside her, quiet, watching, older than his years.

That Diwali, the only light in the house was hope. Hope that Meera would live. Every diya was a prayer. Every chant was a quiet plea: Let her live. That's all we ask.

And now, things were different.

Outside her room, the house was moving again. Voices rose and fell. Fresh flowers lined the puja room. Plates of sweets passed from hand to hand. The doorbell kept ringing. Relatives, neighbours, and old friends arrived with moist eyes and open arms. They weren't celebrating a festival; they were celebrating her.

"Is it Diwali today?" Baba asked, his eyes gleaming. "It certainly feels like it."

Maa rolled laddoos with a rhythm Meera hadn't seen in months. "Today is our Diwali," Maa said. "We'll decorate the house, feed the poor, and go to the temple together." She meant every word.

Marigold garlands hung from the doorways. Diyas lit up the corners. Rekha Bua gave orders from the kitchen. The cook worked quickly, flipping *puris* in hot oil. And the house began to glow, not only with lights but also with something softer.

Love.

Meera wanted to stop them. Tell them to rest, to slow down. But how could she? Not when she saw Baba smiling like that. Not when Maa's voice had its music again. Not when Raju—sweet, serious Raju—was running through the house, stealing sweets, and laughing like a little boy again.

So, she let them be. She sat there watching them, letting it all wash over her.

Because the illness hadn't just lived inside her; it had touched them all. Every prayer they had whispered. Every smile they had hidden. Every night they had stayed awake just to listen to her breathe.

And now, this one piece of news—the one they had prayed for and feared they'd never hear—had brought them back to life.

Their joy wasn't for Diwali. It was for Meera. Her survival. Her return. She was healing, too, though not all at once. Her body was still weak. Her hair hadn't grown back yet, but it would. Her strength hadn't returned, but it would. It would all take time. But watching them laughing, cooking, and decorating, all for her, she felt something return. Something slow and quiet. A sense that she was still here. Still herself. She felt alive.

She stood and looked at herself in the mirror. The face staring back was hers, but it wasn't the same. It was not marked by illness alone but shaped by the quiet strength of survival.

The world was moving again.

And Meera, still tired, still finding her way, was ready to move with it, not because the pain had disappeared, but because the light had returned.

It wasn't Diwali, but it felt like Lord Rama had come home.

Not with drums and fireworks but quietly, in the form of hope, in her father's eyes, in the rhythm of her mother's hands, in Raju's laughter echoing down the hall.

With the morning sun, something settled inside her—a decision not spoken out loud but steady and sure.

It was time. Time to return to herself, to the world she had stepped away from.

Not just to rooms and routines, but to the people she had distanced, gently and silently, when her pain had become too heavy to carry with company.

To Pooja, who had called so many times before giving up. To Aman, whose name still lived silently somewhere inside her, untouched by bitterness.

To her work, which once gave her purpose before everything had come to a stop.

To the small joys—the corner tea stall, the smell of rain on warm soil, the rustle of papers on her desk, the smell of fresh ink on freshly printed scripts.

Even if things had changed.

Even if she had changed.

She didn't know how to begin.

Or what she would say.

But she was ready.

One call.

One message.

One step at a time.

She didn't need to arrive anywhere.

She just had to begin.

A sudden ringing broke the stillness.

Meera reached for the landline, her fingers brushing the receiver like muscle memory.

"Hello? Meera… it's me."

Pooja's voice spilled into the room, warm, sharp, familiar. It moved through the silence like sunlight on closed eyelids. Unchanged by distance. Unbothered by months of silence.

Meera closed her eyes and just listened.

After weeks of test results and patched prayers, after all that quiet pain, this ordinary moment felt like a gift.

"I have some amazing news," Pooja said, her voice lifting. "Aman has cleared the civil service exam. Not just the written. He has aced the interview, too."

Meera didn't speak at first.

Her breath held still, then slipped out slowly.

A small smile rose, the kind that comes from deep knowing.

"I knew he would," she said softly. "I always knew."

Pooja laughed, not with joy, but with edges. Sharp, deliberate, almost practised. "I thought you'd be in your new home by now… with your husband. But here you are, still answering landlines like a scene from the past."

She paused. Her next words were smooth, rehearsed, like lines read too many times.

"Well, of course, you're married to a civil servant now. The same dream you had with Aman. Just a different face. I'm sure he's kind, maybe even loves you. But he's not Aman. If only you'd waited, Meera. You could've had the certainty and the love."

Meera took a breath, shallow, then deeper.

Her voice was calm, almost too calm. "Sometimes," she said, "life doesn't wait for us to choose perfectly. And sometimes… love means letting go." She didn't say more. Not because there wasn't more to say, but because there was too much.

The nights when pain hollowed her out. The mornings that arrived without light. The fear, the silence, the decisions no one saw.

But this wasn't the moment for that. Not over a call. Not in words that couldn't carry the weight. Some things needed eyes not ears, presence not distance.

So, she stayed quiet. She held the receiver a little longer, as if silence could speak in ways her voice never could.

Pooja spoke again, too quickly. "Oh, and by the way, you'll be getting another surprise soon. Just wait for it."

Meera opened her mouth to ask, to wonder, but the call was disconnected. She sat there, phone still pressed against her ear, though the line had long gone still.

Outside, the light shifted. The peepal leaves fluttered softly, as if nodding at her, knowing something.

Aman had made it. He had reached the place they once dreamed of together, the one they had painted with words and late-night wishes.

Meera smiled because she had made it, too. Not to a title or a rank, but to life. Back from the edge. She was still here. Still breathing. Still healing.

And maybe this moment, this quiet, golden sliver of now, belonged to them both, in very different ways.

She didn't know which felt heavier: his success or her survival. But both were real. Both were hard-earned. And both were enough.

Two days later, as the morning sun spilled gold across the floor, Baba called out from the veranda.

"Meera, the postman is here. There's something for you."

She pulled her shawl tighter and stepped outside. The envelope was thick, cream-coloured, with no sender's name, only her own, written in neat, deliberate handwriting she knew too well.

She opened it slowly. The card inside caught the light, gold lettering pressed into soft matte:

*Pooja weds Aman.*

Her breath caught.

And for a moment, everything stilled—the sound of birds, the rustle of leaves, even her own heartbeat. The names blurred. The paper felt heavier than it was. Something else fell from the envelope, a folded note. She wiped her eyes with the back of her hand and picked it up, fingers trembling.

Three words, written in Pooja's hand:

Just for information.

She read them again. And again. As if a different meaning might appear the third time.

Behind her, Baba asked, "Whose wedding is it, Meera?"

She cleared her throat, the words slow to arrive. "Pooja's."

He turned a page in his newspaper. "And the groom?"

She paused. "Aman."

He looked up. "What does he do?"

"It's not mentioned," she said in a low voice.

"She didn't tell you?"

A shrug. "We haven't talked much. She's been… busy."

Baba nodded, eyes drifting back to the paper.

Meera walked away quietly, the card still in her hand. Inside her room, she closed the door behind her and sank to the floor.

The invitation was pressed against her chest, the note still between her fingers. The tears came quietly, like the kind that had nowhere left to go.

It wasn't the wedding that undid her or even the truth that Aman had chosen someone else. It was the way it ended, not with anger, not with a last conversation, but with three words:

Just for information.

She knew they weren't Pooja's alone. They belonged to Aman, too.

His silence had been speaking for months, but now it was official. Sealed. Delivered.

There was a time she thought their story might circle back—a slow reunion over tea, maybe laughter, maybe something softer than forgiveness. But this… this was not that. This was final.

She hadn't just lost him. She had become less than memory—not a chapter, not a footnote, but a whisper at the bottom of the page.

Still, she couldn't hate him.

But the ache stayed. The ache of a silence too loud to forget, of being left without even the dignity of a goodbye.

The wedding day had arrived.

Somewhere in Delhi, amid the soft hum of Sanskrit chants and the steady shimmer of chandeliers, Aman and Pooja were becoming husband and wife.

Meera wasn't there to see it, but she could picture it.

Pooja, bright and radiant, wrapped in deep red, the kind of red that demanded to be noticed. Aman, likely in ivory or something pale and quiet, the kind of tone that asked nothing of anyone. She imagined them that way—her, fire, him, steady flame.

Meera had seen it long before this day—the way Pooja's laughter pulled Aman out of his silences, the way his calm met her chaos and didn't flinch. She had seen how they balanced each other, not perfectly, but naturally, like breath and stillness, like the sea meeting the shore.

And maybe, even then, something in her had known, not out of jealousy or fear, but from that quiet, unmistakable place in the heart that sees truth before the mind is ready.

And yet, it still hurt because now it was real. And that small voice inside her, the one she had silenced for so long, spoke again:

It was never meant to be me.

A thought slipped through, soft and sudden. What if she had told them? About the illness. The fear. The way her body felt like borrowed time. What if she hadn't disappeared behind silence, thinking she was protecting him?

Would the *mandap* have been hers to stand under? Would the card have read *Meera weds Aman*?

The ache came slowly, then steadily.

But she knew that even if she had told him, it would have been unfair to give him a choice shaped by fear, by the shadow of loss. He had been standing on the edge of everything he had worked for. She didn't want to drag him back into her storm.

So, she had let him go. Not because she stopped loving him, but because she loved him enough not to hold him back.

And now, he had arrived. In the life they once dreamed of. Full and certain. Living the version of a future they had built in whispers and half-sketched plans.

Could she still ask: What about me?

No. That wouldn't be fair either.

She had once believed that letting go was the most loving thing she could do. That stepping away would give him space to grow. But maybe it wasn't her silence that helped him. Maybe it was Pooja.

Maybe when Meera let go of his hand, it was Pooja who reached for it and held on. Through doubt. Through worry. Through the dark days that Meera never saw. Maybe it was Pooja's presence that steadied him. Her belief that built him back. Her love that stayed.

If that was the truth—if Pooja had been the one to carry him forward—how could Meera question it?

Aman had found love. And now, she had to find peace.

She was not his now. Maybe she never really was. And accepting that might be the only way to begin again.

She had once told herself that love wasn't ownership. That time could stretch the space between two people until even memories couldn't close the gap.

She believed she had made peace with it.

But now that he belonged to someone else, now that his voice, his laughter, his breath lived in someone else's life, it hurt in places she hadn't named.

The thought of him lying beside another, whispering the same softness he once gave her, was a different kind of grief. One with no shape, no sharpness. Just a quiet ache.

She had let go. But this was the last thread. This moment. This final breath between what was and what would never be again.

And if it had to be someone else, she was glad it was Pooja.

She matched Aman in ways Meera never could. She had always known that.

A leaf floated down beside her, golden-edged, trembling. It settled in her lap, quiet and whole.

She traced its veins with her fingertip.

It had once belonged to the tree, but now, it didn't. Its time had ended. And still, it was beautiful.

She reached out and touched the bark of the old peepal tree near her. Rough, patient, constant. It had stood through seasons. It had watched her leave and return, break and begin again. It had held her story, even when she couldn't. And now, it would see her rise.

Because life, she knew now, could slip away in a single breath. And she wasn't done breathing yet.

Inside, Baba folded his newspaper and looked toward the courtyard. "She's not the same," he said quietly. "She doesn't argue anymore or laugh like before."

Maa's voice was hushed. "I've prayed in every temple. Lit every diya. And still…"

"She's been through more than we understand," Baba said. "Cancer doesn't just leave the body. It lingers. In shadows, in the mind. Some scars are seen. Others stay hidden."

Maa looked down. "Maybe if we find her a good match, she'll feel whole again."

"She'll marry when she's ready," Baba said gently. "We have to trust her timing."

"And if it's too late by then?" Maa whispered.

Baba didn't answer.

Meera didn't hear them. She sat beneath the tree, her thoughts scattered across time.

The road ahead would be slow, maybe even lonely. Not just because Aman had chosen another path, but because she was learning how to live in a world that had kept going without her.

Still, she breathed in.

There would be other moments. Quiet ones. Unexpected ones. She was no longer waiting for what had passed. She was choosing something else. She would apply for new work, piece together a new rhythm. She might always carry a small ache for Aman and Pooja, but she would carry it lightly.

Because life was too sacred to live in the shadows of what could've been.

She was moving forward, not fully steady, but sure enough.

And maybe, that was its own kind of grace.

The editorial office moved like a slow wave—phones ringing, pages rustling, voices humming low. Meera sat at her desk, a half-drunk cup of chai beside her, paper clippings and proofs scattered like fallen leaves.

Words had always been her refuge, a place she could enter when the world became too sharp. Now, they were helping her build again, one sentence at a time.

She had promised herself she would start over. And she was trying.

Some days began with purpose—a story idea that felt right, a walk that cleared her head. Other days came heavy—a forgotten tune on the radio, a jacket hanging by the door, the sound of laughter that wasn't his.

The past had a way of returning. Not loudly. Just… in small, quiet slips.

Sometimes, when the ache came suddenly and strangely, she'd find her fingers hovering near the landline, thinking of calling Pooja. Just to hear her voice. Just to ask how he was. But that was another world now, one she had stepped out of.

She reminded herself that this wasn't about them. It never was. It was about her, a promise made in the silence of one long night: to move forward, not away, to write, to live.

The job at the magazine wasn't a distraction. It was a kind of scaffolding, something that held her steady. She wasn't chasing the biggest cover stories or photo spreads. She wanted stories that breathed, stories with bruises and light.

Her assignments took her everywhere. Cafés that smelled of burnt coffee. Halls filled with noise and typewriters. Back streets and art rooms. She spoke to dreamers and drifters. To people who had lost and kept walking anyway.

She listened with the kind of silence only those who've known silence carry. Most stories didn't make it to print. But they stayed. In her chest. In the pages of her notebook. In the spaces between her thoughts.

On weekends, she went to Sanjivani, an NGO for cancer patients. What began as a way to stay busy had become something sacred. She didn't talk about her own story. She didn't need to. She simply showed up. Sat with people. Poured tea. Held hands.

There was a boy who sang to his mother as the drip ticked on. A man who talked about reopening his vegetable shop as if it were still waiting for him. A woman who gripped Meera's wrist with words she couldn't say out loud.

She didn't try to fix anything. She just stayed.

In their fear, she saw her own, not in the details, but in the shape of it. The heaviness. The trying.

Three years had passed since her remission. It wasn't something she celebrated. It was more like a date she carried in her body. Her muscles still stiffened without warning. Fatigue arrived on good days. But she no longer fought it. She listened. She rested. And then, she moved again.

Her hair had grown back, thicker, darker. She didn't chase beauty anymore, but sometimes when she looked in the mirror, she saw someone she knew. That quiet recognition felt like a kind of return.

At Sanjivani, she met people who redefined strength, like the woman in the red saree, bald, limping, laughing, who spoke of love like it was an old friend who still wrote letters. That kind of grace stayed with Meera.

She began to understand healing wasn't going back to the girl she had been; it was becoming someone new. Someone softer. Someone who still held beauty, even with the scars.

This life wasn't what she'd planned. But it was real, made not from fantasy, but from choice.

Some evenings were still long, still quiet in a way that pressed against the ribs. She missed the voices that had once filled her space. She missed the ease of being held. But she didn't live in 'what ifs' anymore.

She showed up. Fully. Some days tired, some days sure. But always whole.

Once in a while, a smell or a line of music would pull her back to a moment, a touch, a laugh. To Aman. To Pooja. But not with regret, not even sadness. Just… memory.

The heart doesn't always ask for permission. It remembers in its own time.

Still, she had come far.

She had a job she believed in, people she showed up for, a life she had shaped with her own hands.

And yes, there were nights when a soft space inside her stirred, a space that once bloomed in the presence of love.

Her mother would ask gently, "Don't you want someone to come home to?"

And maybe she did.

But not yet.

She wasn't waiting for a perfect love or a promise.

She had already learned the most important thing—to come home to herself.

She sometimes thought of the peepal tree—how it had stood still while she found the strength to move on.

Maybe when love returned, it would look different. Not fireworks but a steady flame. Not someone to complete her, but someone to meet her where she stood. As she was.

Enough.

She let out a breath and turned back to the page.

There were stories still waiting.

And she was walking toward them, open, steady, and whole.

Meera adjusted the pleats of her saree. The deep blue draped over her shoulder like dusk. She wore no jewellery, just a thin bracelet on one wrist and a leather-strap Titan watch on the other.

Her father had given it to her the day she took up this job. "Time heals everything," he had said, strapping it around her wrist. "Today, I give you time. Your own time."

She had smiled then, not knowing how his words would linger, folding themselves into the silence of her days. Time had passed. It had softened sharp corners, dulled what once hurt. But here, now, waiting in this silence, she wasn't sure if time had healed anything at all.

Even before he entered, she knew it would be him.

The interview letter had said it clearly: Aman Verma, IAS.

But knowing is different from facing.

You imagine the moment. You rehearse the lines. You tell yourself you're ready. But when the past walks back in wearing a pressed suit and silence, you feel the ground shift.

A faint ticking filled the room.

Then, the door creaked open.

She turned.

Aman stepped in.

And the breath she didn't know she was holding let itself go.

He had changed.

The boy she remembered—kind, warm—was gone. Before her stood a man carved by time. Slim, still, in a tailored suit. His eyes behind thin-rimmed glasses were steady and unreadable. Something inside her stirred, the old ache blooming again, quietly, like a bruise beneath the skin.

She had told herself she could handle this. But some part of her—quiet, trembling—had hoped it wouldn't be him. Another part had longed for it to be him.

Yes, it was him. Just as she had expected. Just as she had feared.

Their eyes met.

She searched his face for the boy she had once loved, the one she had walked away from without a proper goodbye. But all she saw was a man, shaped by absence.

Maybe time had changed her, too.

He walked toward her with slow and measured steps. His presence filled the room.

"Ms Meera Kapoor," he said, his voice calm, detached.

Her name, on his tongue, sounded foreign. Formal.

He had never called her that before.

She wanted to say just "Aman".

But she didn't.

"Mr Aman Verma," she replied, her smile polite, distant.

Two names. Two strangers.

He nodded and took the seat across from her. The silence that followed was not awkward but full. Dense with memory.

She reached for her notes, straightened them too many times. She needed something to hold on to.

"Shall we begin?"

The interview unfolded in a structure. Questions. Answers. Each sentence carefully shaped, each thought measured. He spoke like someone used to being watched. Composed. Articulate. Distant.

She listened, too still, hearing not just the words but what lived between them—the breath, the pauses, the weight.

She waited for a crack in his voice, a shift in his eyes. A story he wouldn't tell but couldn't help carrying. Maybe a mention of someone he once loved. Maybe a wound stitched, but still sore.

And in those silences, she heard it.

Something unfinished.

Maybe he had changed.

Maybe he had healed in ways she couldn't see. Maybe he, too, had learned how to walk around a scar quietly.

Still, she found herself looking for him, the small things—the way he adjusted his cuff, the crease between his brows. So much had changed. But some pieces remained.

The way he looked at her, his gaze still and steady.

Still capable of making her heart lose its rhythm.

She sat across from him, inches away, knowing he belonged to someone else.

Pooja.

The name passed through her like a hush.

Was she going to walk in?

Would she see her, even for a second?

She braced for it. A meeting of eyes. A silence exchanged.

And then, they reached the question she had rehearsed and dreaded.

Her voice almost caught.

"Your work demands so much," she said, trying to sound neutral. "Does it…leave space for a personal life?"

He adjusted his cuff.

"Some would say that," he replied, offering a small smile. "But in my case, there isn't much of a balance to maintain."

She blinked, confused.

"What do you mean?"

His voice softened, just enough to stir the air between them.

"I chose to stay focused on work," he said. "Some hearts are meant to walk alone. Even if they once beat together."

Her breath stilled.

Then, without planning it, her question slipped out, halting, uncertain.

"And… your wife? Pooja…?"

A pause. A flicker in his eyes—surprise, maybe. Something unguarded.

"Pooja is happily married," he said quietly.

Then, before the meaning could settle, he added, "But not to me."

"What?" she asked dazedly.

"She's married," he said again. "Just not to me."

"I—" Meera blinked. "But…the card. I remember seeing it. It said 'Pooja weds Aman'."

Aman let out the faintest smile, not bitter, just old.

"Yes. But I'm not the only Aman in the world."

He paused, then said gently, "She married Aman Rana."

The air left her. She sat very still.

Of course.

Not her Aman.

Pooja Aman Rana.

And suddenly, everything rearranged itself—the way Pooja had once pulled away, the quiet distance she carried into the room, the lunches she began to skip, the days she seemed elsewhere.

Aman Rana. Their old team lead. Always dependable. Always present.

How hadn't she seen it? She had. She just hadn't let herself see it.

She let out a soft, half-laugh, almost like disbelief. "All this time…"

Aman leaned forward just a little, his voice low.

"Would it have made a difference… if you'd known?"

She didn't answer.

Because the answer was yes.

Yes, it would have changed everything.

Maybe she wouldn't have left so quietly.

Maybe the day she was declared cancer-free, she would have run to him.

But she said nothing.

She couldn't. Not now.

This wasn't a moment for falling apart.

This was still an interview.

She stood up, gently gathering her file.

"Thank you for your time, Mr Aman Verma."

He stood up too, mirroring her restraint.

Their eyes met one last time. Still. Searching.

And in that look, something flickered. Not goodbye.

Not quite.

She turned to leave.

And for the first time in years, it didn't feel like walking away.

It felt like walking toward something.

And she wasn't afraid to find out what that might be.

# Epilogue

Meera stood beneath the old peepal tree, a place she had returned to time and again. In silence. In confusion. In pain.

She never knew what brought her here each time. But today, she did.

The tree didn't ask anything of her. It didn't speak or offer comfort. It just stood. Still. Watching the world pass. People came with their stories, left with their silences, and the tree stayed the same. Just there.

She once thought love meant protection. That by hiding the truth from Aman, she was shielding him from pain. That if she held the pen, the story would hurt less.

But now, standing here, she saw it for what it truly was.

She hadn't been saving him.

She had been deciding for him.

Not because she meant harm, but because she was scared.

Scared of the truth.

Scared of what it would break.

Scared he wouldn't understand.

But love isn't about fear. It isn't about control.

Love isn't possession. It's presence.

Love is telling the truth, even when it's heavy.

Love is letting someone choose, even if it breaks you.

Maybe one day, she would go back to Aman, not to explain but to say:

I thought I was protecting you. But I see now… I wasn't.

I was taking away your freedom to choose.

And for that, I'm sorry.

And if they ever found their way to each other again, it would be different.

It wouldn't be one person writing the story.

It would be two people, standing side by side, with their own pages, their own voices.

Real love isn't about writing someone else's story.

It's about standing with them, page after page, word after word…

And letting the ending unfold together.

The peepal tree whispered above her, leaves moving gently in the breeze.

She smiled.

This time, she wasn't trying to write anything.

She was just listening.

She understood now…

It wasn't her story to write.

## Author's Note

Some stories live with us long after the last word is written. This one—Meera's—taught me more than I had set out to discover.

It reminded me of the quiet strength it takes to let go, of how love, when bound by fear or control, loses its truth.

There is something powerful in watching someone choose their own path, even when it's not the one we would have chosen for them.

In Meera's need to protect, to steer, she forgot that the story was never hers to shape but only to witness, only to love, only to accept.

And so, this reflection remains:

Some stories are not ours to write.
They are simply written in the stars.
Stories, like roots, run deep.
They twist, they turn, they stretch, they grow,
But they are never ours to control.
Like the *peepal* tree, standing still and wise,
We cannot shape the path of another's rise.
For every tale has its own course,
And in the end, it is not our force,
But the freedom to choose, to fall or fly,
That gives each story its meaning, it's why.
So let it be, let them be,
The ones who choose their destiny.
For this, I've learned, in the silence of time—

This was never my story to write.

To every reader holding someone else's story gently in their hands—this is for you.

With love,
Anju Dahiya